Nathan

Nathan

Hemenway Stephens

To order additional copies of this book, contact:
Xlibris LLC
1-888-795-4274
www.Xlibris.com
Orders@Xlibris.com
551092

For Joe, of course

An Elephant's New Life,
The Making of the Theater at St. Bernard's,

and

A Modest History of New York City at the End of the
Second Millennium

by

Nathan Emmanuel

Preamble

"I'm just so concerned about the *title*," I said woefully.

"The title?" Morgan asked.

"Yes. It's so cumbersome."

"I would say instead *encompassing*," countered Abby.

"What do you think of my flyer, Evelyn?" asked Arnold as he passed out coffee and banana-nut bread.

Evelyn began looking for her reading glasses in her capacious handbag, finding instead a long-lost hat, which she placed on her head with triumphant joy.

"This bread really rocks, Arnold," said Cookie.

"Thanks, Cookie," said Arnold. "Nathan, maybe you shouldn't worry about the title so much. Maybe you should call it *Reality: The Next Step* or *Sidewalks Give Perspective*. You know, give a title that has nothing to do with what it is and let everyone work it out for themselves."

"That's a cool idea. You know, like chocolate mousse," offered Cookie, her eyes—as always—especially luminous whenever she attempted abstraction.

"Why, Arnold, it's absolutely lovely," said Evelyn, having found her reading glasses and now gazing at the daring magenta flyer. "But I don't think my name should be so big."

"But you're the big name, Evelyn."

"Oh lord. No one remembers *Kiss Me Once Kiss me Twice*, Arnold."

"They will," said Arnold solemnly as Evelyn quickly turned away to wipe away a small tear.

"Morgan, you are my mentor and guide, my friend. What do you suggest?" I asked.

"You know what strikes me as particularly interesting about this confab, Nathan?" asked Morgan as he looked upon this odd grouping, all of us gently thoughtful, quiet, happy, drinking superb coffee from Zimbabwe in the lovely sepia-toned light that flooded Morgan's apartment every evening about six—relative, of course, to the earth's rotation and the tilt of its axis.

"What?" I asked hopefully, remembering the time I almost stepped into my saucer not so long ago at a pivotal moment of awakening.

"You've created it."

It was an astonishing moment, dear reader, one filled with both a warmth and grandeur that suddenly pierced the tangles of reality, the multiplicities of time and space.

And so it is with some relief that I realize it is always good to title a thing for what it is, no matter the encumbrance. In that way, you can return again and again to remind yourself where you are going, in order to discover—with all its warmth and grandeur—it may be where you have always been.

Another Preamble

"Wait a minute," I said. "Why do I need another preamble?"

"Because I just thought of something, and I speak for every single one of us when I say that," said Evelyn who had settled down to her electric keyboard, which she carried everywhere.

The room quieted down, with Cookie especially awed by the fact that, unbeknownst to herself, she had actually thought of something.

"Well, all right," I said. "But I hate to keep the reader waiting."

"Well, Nathan, what I am wondering is this." Evelyn paused a moment, looking over a well-thumbed piece of sheet music. "When *exactly* are you writing this?"

"When?" I temporized.

"Yes. I mean is the book finished yet?"

"Oh. No. Not exactly. I just got the idea for the title and then doubts crept in and so on and so forth and I needed to hash it out as they say."

"*Hash!*" said Cookie. "Another example!"

"So we don't know if any of this really worked out. I mean, if any of us actually *got* here, do we?" Evelyn faced me now with both a gentle challenge and deep concern.

Morgan and Abby stared at each other, uncertain. Arnold glanced over at Evelyn and then down at the flyer for his new show. Even Cookie froze, her gaze stilled upon her lovely feet encased in sandals. I looked upon Morgan's beautiful home, at this collection of gentle individuals, at Arnold's banana-nut bread, and finally at my good friend who eyed me with, as always, compassion.

And as the lovely sepia-toned light dissolved into night, drawing a curtain on an ending now no longer certain, I realized I had finally encountered that one dreadful and necessary component for which any writer would sell his soul.

Suspense.

Genealogy

I am a toy elephant, cut and sewn by Elvira Haines née Patterson in August of 1950 for her freshly born baby, Emma Louise, who—even in the vague blurry days of early life—recognized a kindred spirit and clutched me intensely from that moment onward.

At the age of five, Emma Louise changed my name from "Ewephant" to the considerably more specific "Nathan Emmanuel Christ," although the "Christ" was used only between the two of us after it caused a bit of a ruckus in the household. I feel it only fair to add, however, that I did see a clear brief sign of approbation in her father's eye.

I stand nine inches high from my foot to the top of my head, with a gentle slope downward to my tailbone. My length, from bow to stern, measures twelve and a half inches. I have brown button eyes—one recently replaced after visits to numerous button shops throughout the city, for I was assured by my friend and mentor that my remaining eye was not simply brown but, rather, "the color of root beer in the glass that the guest leaves." (This somewhat offhand paraphrase of dear Emily Dickinson gave me great joy, for it suggested that my friend and mentor might have a love of reading comparable to my own.) I am fashioned from leatherette—one of several suggested fabrics including calico, flannel, gingham, and of course, the ubiquitous mattress ticking.

Today, seamstresses are to be found in the most unexpected of personalities (professors, theatrical artists, dental hygienists) as easily as the traditional housewife and young mother, and as would be expected, they choose such unexpected materials as velvet, lace, vivid sateens, and so on.

While I try to cast no initial judgment, I am reminded of dear Oscar Wilde who said "Only shallow people do not judge by appearances," and thus it is with a somewhat jaded eye that I note this young breed fashioned with lace overlay, ears lined with silk and pearl buttons for eyes. What their futures are no one can say, but I dearly hope their lives go no further than a lady's dressing table. Not for them the infant's eternal drool, the toddler's mighty tug!

It has always been a source of pride to me that Mrs. Haines's Fabric of Choice for myself was her daughter Emma Louise's baby mattress from her beautifully fashioned cradle, and that Mrs. Haines also spent long tedious hours fashioning a simple yet tasteful piping to accent my two major seam lines—for during our bleakest hour we reflect upon the fabric of which we are made, hoping that it is stern enough to see us through the difficult times.

The aforementioned baby mattress had its own history, having been Mrs. Haines's mattress when she was the infant Elvira Patterson, only daughter of Mr. and Mrs. Wentright Patterson. Samuel and Mathew who preceded her by two and four years respectively also did their tours of duty upon this selfsame mattress, and while the mattress was tenderly wiped clean with motherly devotion, I have found great comfort in keeping company with the infantile secretions of this earlier generation.

Lest the reader wonder how exactly a mattress survives such arduous use long enough to become the Fabric of Choice for such a one as me, let me mention that while a cradle may add a tender visual element to hearth and home, the infant often becomes frantic as it sways uncontrollably, knocking its soft head against the oaken sides. It soon screams for an end to its misery, and the cradle then becomes a simple yet homey repository for skeins of yarn, toys, and the odds and ends of life that have no function yet remain extremely necessary.

As I have been encouraged by my Patron to present not only a chronology but a personal perspective, I will say here that it has been my misfortune to meet several thick-headed adults who were no doubt left too long helpless victims to the cradle's mighty sway, and having survived such a hapless and unfortunate introduction to the world, are now grimly uncompromising, as if the most ordinary hard-knocks of life harbinger a return to that eternity of helpless inertia.

The cradle which held the mattress from which I was created was fashioned by Emmet Haines, husband to Elvira, who insisted that he make a new cradle for his own progeny, perhaps in his last gesture of independence. Emmet was a generous and romantic man who had the great misfortune to have left his love of cabinetry to work at the Bristol Savings and Loan, the president of which was Elvira's father, Mr. Wentright Patterson. Permit me, dear reader, to share the budding romance of Emmet and Elvira as I have come to imagine it.

> Emmet Haines, a generous and romantic man with a genuine love for cabinetry, has picked up his mother's ormolu clock from Nutmeg Valley Clockworks at 27 Walnut Street, where it had been sent for cleaning, and now thinks a grilled cheese and a cup of joe at Gabby's Diner over on Main Street might be the perfect thing.

> Elvira Patterson has dropped into her father's office at Bristol Savings and Loan on Main Street as she often does when she comes to town. Wentright Patterson is considered by most an august and forbidding gentleman who—upon his august and forbidding arrival at the bank each morning—makes even the

most seasoned teller nervously recount his transaction. However, to Elvira he is her beloved Papa whom she can charm even on the busiest of days, perching atop his desk and making him laugh in spite of his over-full schedule. Realizing suddenly that she is late for a dress-fitting at Madame LaRue's at 44 Walnut Street, Elvira kisses her father good-bye and briskly sets off down Main Street, breathing in the fulsome spring air and admiring the overnight blossoming of lilacs and forsythia.

Thereupon a serendipitous collision on the corner of Walnut and Main. Apologies, a sudden locking of eyes, quick intakes of breath; Elvira drops her gloves, both reach, they touch; an inexplicable urge on Elvira's part for a grilled cheese sandwich and a cup of joe; hands touching again as both reach for the cream, laughter, then a slow walk back to the bank to meet Elvira's father who immediately finds Emmet amiable and keen-witted. The position of bank manager is offered, which Emmet cannot refuse, followed by a wedding large enough to cover two pages of the *Bristol Gazette*. A child is born, six years pass, and then suddenly (but not inexplicably) Emmet disappears.

I say "not inexplicably" for it was during my later difficult times in dim attic light, when I had many years to peruse a myriad of dusty books and ruminate over meanings found therein, that I began to understand one of many simple truths: if our outer lives do not reflect our inner desires, a moment arrives when life will change forever.

For Emmet should have escaped years earlier and bundled his wife and child and myself into his 1949 Ford to head for a new land. As he did not, his moment came in the person of Mrs. Pentwhistle, of 41 East Pine, who hired him to do some cabinetry work in her kitchen. What happened *precisely* in that kitchen, no one will ever know. However, the rumor, the suspicion, the ice-blue gaze of Grampy Patterson (I employ the nomenclature of my dear Emma Louise), and the inexorable life of adding machines, interest compounded quarterly, and bank reconciliations all contributed to the flight of that romantic man to Florida, where he was last seen leading a small tour through the Everglades in canoes of his own fashioning.

Tender Elvira! How often I wished to turn back that ormolu clock which rested with me through the long dark times, its charming face having become only a painful memory for you, to turn it back to the day when Emmet fled. Could you have found the courage to forgive him and flee with him, so that the future might have found us all paddling into a brave new world? For would that not have been preferable to a life spent hovering among platitudes meant to hide the shame of a broken marriage during an infinity of afternoon teas?

What would our ensuing story have been?

But is it late afternoon already! The pitcher of daisies tells me so. When I settled here at the Gateway 2000 P575-75 megahertz Pentium chip, 4 megabytes EDO memory with a 1.4-megabyte disc drive, 1 GB, seven bays, laser printer 4-L, CD-ROM built in, 16-bit sound card—the lovely bouquet was bathed in a full shaft of sunlight and now lies in shadow.

How time, which hung so heavily in that old attic creaking with age, now vanishes as I relive and recount!

I wonder if time has flown so completely from me only to sit immovable on the back of some poor creature who wonders now, in the dark attic of his own soul, if time has stopped for him? I pray no! I say "Courage to all who wait in dim attic light! All is not lost!"

I look forward to Morgan's return, for one's heart does not always step lightly into the past, and our evenings—which consist of reading quietly over cocoa and biscotti—are a balm to my soul. Morgan is most generous with his capacious library, and I have chosen a slim volume entitled *Our Town*, which I assume will give me useful tips on restaurants, museums, and out-of-the-way places in this great city.

But what actually delivered me into A New Life with this Gentle Man of a certain age who has his own quiet dreams and hopes which, as yet, remain a mystery to me?

Dare I say to you, a reader I have known for even less time than this Gentle Man—dare I say to you that what has delivered me is love? For Emma Louise loved me with a ferocity and possession from the moment the last thread was clipped. I can still feel the muscle of her young elbow as she cradled me each night in her arms, as she herself was cradled in the arms of Morpheus.

A daring child, only she could challenge Grampy Patterson, for she had his jaw. And though I believe him to be a classic example of the "infant left too long swaying in the cradle," he was also keen enough to know when he had met his match as he had once in his youthful Elvira, and thus agreed to Emma Louise's audacious demand that I not only be allowed to sit at the dinner table, but that a place must be set and the maid must serve me (albeit smaller portions) as well. And thus it went—a love which stayed deep, even while it shifted and changed and oft' times seemed lost.

And I do believe that when one loves and *is* loved so fiercely, love sits forever in one's stuffing and one views the world, even in dim attic light, with love.

It is this fact, this life force, which delivered me into the hands of a gentleman of a certain age as he happily perused the offerings of a New York City flea market in late August of 1995.

With my one remaining button eye, I watch him examine a set of piglet salt and pepper shakers, an old radio, and a *Life Magazine* with Jackie Onassis on the cover. Just as he leaves my limited range of vision, his hand is back, he lifts, he smiles, and he calls over to the ancient man behind the table with a bright laugh in his voice, "Who says you cannot go home again?" (Of course I understand the literary allusion. I have been with books now for some thirty years.) And he begins to replace . . . but then suddenly his own bright laughter, his initial impulse merely to partake of hearty banter, is halted as something in *me* reaches out to *him*. Is it that perhaps for a brief, very brief moment, he *did* go home again? And found it welcoming? For in a matter of moments, money is exchanged, I am bundled into a bag and surrounded by sudden sounds of children, dogs and steel-drum bands, I am whisked to my new home.

I am thus delivered into an unhoped-for happiness.

I am reborn.

And tonight, as I read what I now understand to be a *play*, I look up from Emily's third-act speech and gaze out into a quiet night, my heart suddenly filled with compassionate understanding of her stunning declaration: "Oh, Earth, you're too wonderful for anybody to realize you." And I suddenly find the courage to ask the question that I could never ask through all those dreadful dark times.

Where are you now, Emma Louise?

Breakfast

It is early Monday morning and Morgan and I are headed briskly to the Studio Coffee Shoppe. The morning is bright and clear, and I am stuffed happily into Morgan's sport coat pocket, nestled deeply enough to be safe and yet not so deep that I am unable to observe the rich fabric of city life, the scurrying of various hues of people—such variation from what I can dimly recall of Bristol's Barnes Hill, the enclave of the very wealthy and infinitely pale. Morgan calls out happy hellos to various people who dot the landscape—only one of whom I recognize, a gentleman by the name of Mr. Stinker.

"Tinker," Morgan corrects me.

Mr. Tinker, a gypsy.

"Not at all," murmurs Morgan.

I remonstrate slightly, for if the reader will recall, I gathered much information from literature, dictionaries, encyclopedias, thesauri, atlases, farmers' almanacs, how-to books—

"And that is to be commended," Morgan replied. "For the life of the mind is a precious thing. The wisdom of the ages handed down to us is nothing less than miraculous. However, information is not necessarily knowledge, and knowledge is not necessarily wisdom!"

And his eyes sparkle brightly as he holds the door of the Studio Coffee Shoppe for a bulky and silent man who carries some eight bags and four or five aluminum plates, delivering breakfast to the various offices around us. But he is, to me, a frightening man, for his head reminds me of a large turnip. I duck down deeply into the pocket as I am quite skittish by nature.

"Not at all," Morgan repeats gently—for as the reader has perhaps already noted, Morgan has an uncanny ability to respond to my narration before I actually commit it to paper later in the evening. "You have had a long life amid books, clocks, silver tea services, broken vacuum cleaners—"

"Cushions, magazines, shoes, tuxedoes—"

"And therefore—"

"Toasters, costumes, tap shoes—"

"Nathan—"

"Horseshoes, Parcheesi sets—"

"And therefore!" His hand gracefully gestures that his point has been sufficiently illustrated. "You must simply reacquaint yourself with the bluntness, the serendipity, the mystery, the sharp unfolding that is life."

"Hot cereals again for the two of you?" the waitress asked.

"Yes please." Morgan smiled. "And coffee right away."

"Coffee right away," the waitress whispered immediately, with him nodding that she had almost remembered. She turned to me apologetically.

"I just can't remember if you do or do *not* want that pat of butter on your oatmeal."

"None for me," I replied, happy that she remembered that she didn't remember.

The waitress earnestly scribbled on her pad, her face seemingly forever wreathed in a welcoming and homey smile. I realized in this early morning of contentment pending oatmeal that I was in love.

"As for Tinker," Morgan said. "*Tinker* is his last name. He doesn't need to be an actual tinker in order for that to be the case. Thus, the Carpenters were a singing group and, as far as I know, did not actually work with wood. My grandmother's last name was Baker, but there were no piles of gently rising dough anywhere that I can recall. Perry Mason was a lawyer, not a mason, although I am not exactly certain—"

"A mason is a skilled workman who builds with stone or similar material, Morgan, from the Middle English from the Old French. *Freemason*, capitalized, refers to a member of a widespread secret fraternal society called Free and Accepted Masons—although if it's in the dictionary, I am not quite certain how they can continue to believe it's a secret."

I paused as our coffee was placed before us, thinking perhaps that I had been incontinent with information.

"Go on." Morgan smiled, sipping the hot coffee.

"Oh well, then there is the mason bee, a solitary bee that constructs nests of hardened mud and sand."

"And?" Morgan asked.

"*And* well, of course, you know the Mason-Dixon Line, which is the southern boundary line of Pennsylvania and division between the northern and southern states, surveyed by Charles Mason who was an astronomer, of all things, and Jeremiah Dixon."

"It's true then, what they say, Nathan? That an elephant never forgets?"

"It is true, Morgan. It is true and, I might say, a bit of a burden."

Morgan nodded thoughtfully.

"Morgan," I said softly, "I think perhaps I am in love with the waitress."

Morgan raised his eyebrows. "Really?" He turned back to look at her. She glanced over and called out that the cereals would be there very soon. Morgan assured her we were in no hurry now that we had our coffee. I ducked down shyly behind the napkin dispenser.

"I commend your taste, Nathan. But I would encourage you *not* to make your feelings known quite yet."

This surprised me. "Why?" I asked.

"Oh. Well. For a number of reasons."

"Yes?" I leaned forward too eagerly and stepped into my saucer. I sensed suddenly that my natural propensity to collect information was leading me into territory that that could not be classified with the etymology of the word "gossip" or the major reasons for the War of the Roses.

"Well, because—"

Suddenly our bowls of oatmeal were before us, steaming and murky, looking something like an illustration of quicksand that I had seen in the Compton's World Book Encyclopedia, 1965.

"Now I just don't think it's comfortable for you to have to sit on the table like that, so I brought these."

And this paragon of womanhood, who always knew when our coffee cups needed refilling, proceeded to place some five phone books on the booth and myself on top. Dizzy from the attention as well as her cool soft hands, I felt myself begin to swoon. Morgan hurriedly passed me my water glass, and as I composed myself, he easily struck up a conversation, asking how long she had been there ("Twenty years, can you *believe* it?"), how long the cafe itself had been there ("Oh, at least since 1965, but I'm not sure. I could check on that."), if she enjoyed waitressing ("Very much so!"), what the secret was to such excellent coffee ("Cinnamon."), how they got the oatmeal so thick ("Cook it with part water, part milk."), and so on. How I envy his composure, his suavity, his ease!

"Her name," I mouthed silently.

Morgan looked bewildered.

"*Her name.*" I said it as loudly as I dared.

"Oh! Yes! And my name is Morgan, and this is Nathan Emmanuel."

"Very pleased to meet you. My name is Doris."

Doris! Doris! Is there a more beautiful name in the entire world?!

"I'll just let you get on with your cereals now." And she headed off to grace another table with her light, her warmth, and her gentle breakfast suggestions.

"Nathan, eat your cereal while it's still hot," Morgan directed me gently.

I did so without thinking. I watched Doris take the order and disappear into the kitchen. Straining to see her better, I almost toppled off the pile of phone books onto the floor. I righted myself somewhat breathlessly.

"Falling in love can be quite literal," Morgan said, smiling at me over his coffee.

"Yes, I suppose," I answered. "But what are the reasons for not declaring myself, Morgan?" For of all the literature I have perused, I confess I particularly fancied Jane Austen's work as well as the Regency novels, reading them two and three times. I knew from my own life experiences at the Patterson home that life did not necessarily ever bear relationship to literature, especially if life was mid-twentieth century Connecticut. And yet, are not our lives composed of thoughts, hopes, imagination, and dreams which are boundless, in spite of the actual time during and ground upon which our footfalls tread?

"Yes, absolutely," Morgan answered. "And you have an excellent definition of the artistic sensibility, which must infuse one's life, especially if you consider the possibility that we are all artists with our lives being our chef d'oeuvres, as it were."

I concurred with this, although I felt we had wandered from the point.

"But—"

"The chief reason for not declaring yourself immediately is this: you have been stuck in an attic for *thirty years*. Thus, everything seems miraculous: the smell of fresh bread, new buds in spring, rolls of Lifesavers, cups of steaming hot coffee, jaunts in a jacket pocket. Every person will be a foreign land with splendid paths to explore, and possibly—I'm saying *possibly* mind you, with your tendency toward a romantic nature—every woman a queen, a goddess, a paragon of womanhood."

I blushed deeply, hoping it did not penetrate the leatherette.

"Don't misunderstand. I believe love can happen in an instant and a kind of fierce passion reside in you for years." At this moment, Morgan's gaze seemed to shift and, for a moment, he was lost to me, perhaps remembering an instant of his own. "*However*, to act immediately in such situations is not always the best course."

"But what if she is gone from me forever after today?"

"Nathan!" Morgan said sternly. "She has been a waitress here for *twenty* years. In all likelihood, she will not pack up tomorrow!"

I saw his point.

"I am simply encouraging you to relax into the life of the miraculous a bit longer before you make major life decisions."

"Would a month be sufficient, do you think, Morgan?" I asked.

"I think a month—or two or three—is an excellent length of time," Morgan concurred.

"And then I shall declare myself," I said.

"Or not," Morgan added simply.

I chewed thoughtfully on my toast.

"Anything else for you two fellahs?" asked Doris, oblivious of course to the *anything else* I had already begun to imagine.

"Thank you, nothing more," said Morgan, taking the bill and counting out his money.

I noticed that his severely overstuffed wallet affirmed membership to the Metropolitan Museum of Art and the New York Public

Library, permission to drive a vehicle in New York City, several cartoons, and a recipe for clam chowder.

"What are your plans for today, Nathan?" Morgan asked, stuffing that bulky billfold into his back pocket, donning the sports jacket, and placing me into the pocket once more.

"Oh. Well, if it's all right with you, I thought I would settle down to the Gateway 2000 P575, 75 megahertz, Pentium chip—"

"Nathan."

"Four megabytes, EDO memory—"

"Nathan, stop!"

I stopped.

"You can simply say *the computer*."

"Ah."

"Yes."

"The computer."

"Yes, and I'll know what you mean."

"Thank you, Morgan." I was quite happy to discover the cumbersome description could be captured in a noun. "Although wouldn't that allude to a *numerical* activity?" I asked.

"Indeed it would. It does. You make a good point."

"Really?" I asked, surprised. For I thought I had simply asked a question.

"The inventors of the computer certainly had envisioned a far greater future for it than what it has generally become: a quiet typewriter that allows you to dispense with Wite-Out, and the repository for hundreds of video games."

I mused on Morgan's thoughts, for while I certainly could commiserate with inventor's dreams not working out, the fact is I do not possess the fine motor skills needed for the adroit use of Wite-Out. Also, I very much enjoyed a game or two of solitaire whenever I began to tire of my own prose.

Morgan stepped briskly out into the bright morning. Already I had fallen in love, confessed it, incurred moderation, eaten voraciously, adroitly gathered information on the identity of my mentor, and learned a new word. We had traveled a universe over breakfast.

Once again, Morgan held the door for the man with the large turnip head who was returning for another delivery, and in my joy at such a serendipitous bracketing of time, I smiled at him and he at me, and I felt some of my skittish nature begin to evaporate right there at Eighteenth and Eighth.

Work

Today, Morgan asked me if I would like to go to work with him, and I agreed with enthusiastic alacrity, as my only relationship to work had been endless anecdotes about the Bristol Savings and Loan, which frankly had my head nodding at times into the shrimp bisque at the Patterson dinner table.

It seems, for the past week, Morgan has been on vacation, even though it did not in any way compare to the many vacations I had read about, such as in *The Bobbsey Twins Go to the Beach*, Jane Austen's description of Bath, or E. M. Forster's delightful depiction of Florence.

Nor was it like the Pattersons' summer home on Martha's Vineyard, where Emma Louise and I cavorted on the beach throughout the day and sat behind the couch at night with a purloined plate of bridge mix, listening to and recording conversations which Emma Louise had deemed "highly suspicious" and would require decoding for the safety of the Free World.

But Morgan's vacation was a vacation of the mind, where he perused flea markets (as my own life-altering moment would illustrate); visited the Metropolitan Museum on a daily basis; read books on theater history, criticism, and theory; and found interesting new restaurants for lunch.

"Tell me more about those summers at Martha's Vineyard," said Morgan as we jauntily headed over to the National Academy of Drama, an institution which I assumed combined military training with histrionic gesture.

"Oh well, that's about it," I said, jolted suddenly by a cheerful storekeeper's hoisting of a metal wall upward in what sounded like sudden and awful thunder, which disappeared as quickly as it had come. "WHAT WAS—"

"Security," said Morgan. "They keep their businesses safe that way through the night."

"Oh," I said thoughtfully, for I could remember no such characteristic of downtown Bristol.

"Times change," said Morgan.

"Yes they do," I said most emphatically.

"No one knows this better than you," continued Morgan.

"Well, Rip Van Winkle," I offered, needing to be fair.

"Rip Van Winkle!" shouted Morgan a trifle too vehemently, for a Jamaican nanny looked at him in sudden fascination.

Morgan laughed and shook his head. "Nathan. Rip Van Winkle was *fiction.*"

"Yes, of course you're right, Morgan. But remember, literature was my only real company for those many years, and the wall between reality and fiction grew increasingly penetrable until, well . . ."

"Until there was virtually no wall at all."

"Exactly," I said, relieved that there seemed to be no judgment on Morgan's part.

"Judgment?" queried Morgan.

"Yes. You could easily be forgiven for thinking my sometime inability to tell the difference between fiction and reality indicates an unstable mind."

"Pal, the business I'm in *depends* on that inability. And instability," he added thoughtfully.

"Hmmm," I said, thinking this was a path down which I would need to tread more thoroughly. But I was once again becoming mesmerized by the morning bustle of people off to work—men and women in well-tailored dark business suits, carrying attaché cases, speaking on phones. People (actually a disproportionate number of them to my way of thinking) were clearly being pursued by someone. So vehement were they in their pace—

"They're jogging," said Morgan.

"Jogging?"

"Yes. A kinder version of running."

"They are not 'on the lam'?"

"On the lam," repeated Morgan, seeming to savor the words.

"Why would anyone have to run otherwise? Why not choose a brisk pace, or a gentle stroll, or why not just sit in this lovely park and admire the fountain?"

"They're exercising. Getting in shape. Probably none of them are on the lam—if the expensive exercise clothes, headsets, and water bottles are any indication."

"What a terrible thing to do if you don't have to," I murmured sympathetically.

"But what was it like? Being rich on Martha's Vineyard in the sixties?" Morgan said, returning to my earlier recollection.

"Well." I thought a moment. "It was absolutely lovely. During the day, our world was the beach, the ocean, the sand, sand castles, shells, brightly colored umbrellas. Elvira would stay there as long as Emma Louise wanted to play. Elvira was a beautiful woman, graceful, ethereal. After Everett left, she would sit in her beach chair wearing a straw hat with an enormous brim and large sunglasses, just gazing out to sea as if she could see him paddling into the Everglades. Grandfather Patterson had softened considerably, as if somehow he were to blame. He would sit with her quietly holding her hand."

Morgan let the silence of my memory continue, knowing certain memories need silence after they have come up for air.

"But the evenings were my favorite part," I admitted. "The cool interiors, darkness held at bay by lovely lamps inspired by Frank Lloyd Wright, rooms filled with happy, chattering guests in gowns and tuxedos, all of it reflected in the large windows."

"Like *The Great Gatsby*."

"Yes, but not particularly desperate. Just happy. For the most part," I added, remembering Elvira's quiet sadness.

"Yes," said Morgan, nodding. "I should allow the very rich to be very happy."

"And the two of us behind the couch. Emma Louise insisted we sneak downstairs, although I suspect we would have been welcome. She insisted we steal a plate of snacks, even though the servants were quite willing to offer them. She said we had to hone our secret-agent skills. She was most emphatic about that."

Another silence hung between us in the present early-morning bustle.

"I often wondered if she actually ever became a secret agent."

"Possibly." Morgan nodded. "I would have if I hadn't gone into the theater."

"What theater was that, Morgan?" I asked.

"What?"

"Specifically what theater did you walk into that changed your mind about espionage?"

"Oh!" Morgan unaccountably gave another chuckle. "I meant the profession itself."

"Oh!" I echoed, startled. "It's a *profession*." Further explanation was ended by the enthusiastic set of hellos that greeted Morgan as we climbed the few steps into the Academy and entered the lovely interior, which oddly reminded me of the work of Sanford White.

"Not odd at all," said Morgan as we climbed the graceful staircase, weaving our way through clusters of impassioned youth, all of whom seemed to carry overnight bags and who called out "Hey, Morgan!" time and time again. We settled ourselves into a magnificently rundown little room on what might have been the fourth or fifth floor as some eighteen or twenty young people put down their luggage and settled into place, laughing and waving at each other.

"Not odd at all," continued Morgan, "for the Academy used to be a woman's social club, designed by none other than Sanford White."

"NO!" I said, astonished.

"You've got a good eye," said Morgan.

"Sanford White. My god. I'm honored," I said softly.

"Everyone! We begin," said Morgan, seeing that it was exactly nine o'clock. "I'd like to introduce a special visitor today, Nathan Emmanuelle."

"An elephant! Cool," said one young man.

"Adorable!" said a very attractive young woman.

"Is he auditing?" asked another beauty.

"Well, perhaps in a way he is," said Morgan. "Who's up?"

What a curious morning! Each young person came to the front of the room, sat or stood, and then began to speak for several minutes *to no one*, while Morgan wrote on his notepad throughout. Morgan would speak, and then they would speak again—*the exact same words*. I looked at Morgan, wondering if he would say anything; however, perhaps his gentle nature precluded any sort of criticism.

One man talked at length about his revolver; another was justifiably proud of having acquired a Ming Dynasty vase (although he actually held a plastic pitcher, the handle to which was held on with masking tape); one woman gave the most harrowing laugh I have ever heard in my life when she finished speaking; the last young man told us that his wife, who was an Olympic swimmer, had died, and he slept with her bathing suit every night. I was awash in emotion.

"Good work, everyone. See you in a few days."

Everyone happily got up, stretched, drank water, and chatted as they left, acting as if nothing odd had happened at all. I was astonished and, frankly, a bit traumatized by how the morning had gone. Several waved good-bye to me.

"Want to grab some lunch, Nathan?"

"Uh . . . sure," I said. My vagueness was very uncharacteristic, for lunch—indeed, food in general—is a supreme joy for me.

"How are you doing, pal?" Morgan asked as we sat at a small table in a balcony overlooking the salad bar at Ms. Ming's next door.

"Great, Morgan," I said, for the last thing Morgan needed today was to tend to me. These young people, with all of their lives before them, were in far more serious shape than I had ever been or would be.

"The afternoon will be a bit different."

"Oh, good," I said a trifle too quickly.

"You just saw a class of monologues. The afternoon will be scenes. And they will be highly emotional."

"Scenes. Great! I love highly emotional scenes!" I suspected my response was a trifle too enthusiastic.

"Really?" asked Morgan.

I was saved from prevarication by the arrival of an intense woman with skin the color of coffee with a bit of cream and hair so silver, I suspected it was why she needed to wear her sunglasses indoors, for the fluorescent lighting did nothing to diminish its incandescence. She looked up at us and, with great energy, wove her way through. Jostling people choosing from the extraordinary number of items on the salad bar, she stormed the steps up to the balcony and sat down at our table, her bracelets and enormous earrings jangling as she did so. She was swathed in five or six scarves of bright hues and patterns and carried an enormous cobalt-blue handbag the size of a small refrigerator, which she plunked down on the table to rest her arms and head upon. I was mesmerized, for it seemed that we had been suddenly cornered by a famous member of an exotic African tribe.

"Morgan," she said, her voice deep and yet penetrating.

"Veronica," Morgan answered. "I'd like you to meet Nathan."

She peered at me over her sunglasses. Her eyes were impossibly green.

"You're an elephant."

"That's correct," I said cheerfully, relieved that her perceptions were clear and she was fluent in English.

"Welcome to the Academy."

"Thank you."

"Veronica is the head of the Academy," Morgan clarified.

"Oh!" I said, understanding now that there had been method in her extraordinary entrance.

"She actually *is* the Academy, to my way of thinking," added Morgan.

"Oh please," said Veronica. "One has to include things like the president, managing director, bursar, and so on in that statement."

"Actually, one doesn't and one shouldn't. Without you, it would be a factory."

"Well, thank you for that, Morgan." She turned to me. "What do you think so far?"

"Oh. Well. So far, it's been very nice. I love the architecture."

"So do we. But we have to expand."

"Oh," I said. "Really?" I was getting further and further out of my league. "From what I hear, expansion is usually a good thing."

"It is. Absolutely. From an *economic* standpoint."

"Yep," I agreed, nodding my head passionately, as if economics was my field.

"But from the standpoint of *quality*?" And here she flung both hands outward, setting her bangles jangling once again. "Who knows?"

"Indeed." I nodded. "As every great empire has learned all too well."

"Exactly, Nathan! Which is *why*"—and now she turned her brilliant green eyes toward Morgan—"I would like you to consider full-time."

"Thank you, Veronica. But no."

"Please?"

"No. As you remember, I agreed to this job temporarily."

"Yes."

"And that was five years ago."

"Yes. Which is why it's perfect for you to be full-time now."

"I'm not sure I understand the segue."

"Yes you do. You've stayed. You love us."

"I do, Veronica. But I love my independence even more."

"Oh, *that.*" Veronica gazed moodily at the refrigerator section that held an astonishing collection of Gatorade, in colors I never knew existed.

"Will you at least consider it?"

"No."

"Will you at least *say* you'll consider it? You don't have to mean it."

"Sure."

She smiled. "Nice meeting you, Nathan."

"Same here," I said. And I watched her make her reverse journey, this time pausing to buy coffee and speak to various students with warmth and jollity as she stood in line to pay.

We returned to the Academy but now to a different room, slightly larger but just as sweetly dilapidated as the first, for an afternoon of emotional scenes. At the last moment, just before the first pair of actors began, Morgan cautioned me that I might want to shout out something, but to be sure not to. I nodded my head agreeably, as if I knew what he was talking about.

First, a lovely young man and woman seemed to be falling in love on a boat—the young man proposing, the young woman looking radiant but demurring. Morgan said a few things, and they began again. It was the oddest thing, but I suddenly believed they were indeed *on* a boat, and I wanted her to accept his proposal so badly, I almost called out from my shelf, "Take the ring! Take the ring!" But then I remembered my promise to Morgan. I began dreaming of

Doris, wondering if she would consider taking a Circle Line cruise with me some evening.

Then a woman was scrubbing the floor, and when a man came in, she was furious because they had taken the furniture away. He was a taxicab driver, and I thought she should have been a little more sympathetic, as he had worked all day and barely had money for coffee. But then I saw her point because they had children who had rickets because they could not afford oranges. By the end, it seemed someone named Lefty was going to be able to help them, and I was much relieved.

Then a man and woman staggered home from a party, and just as Howard started to leave, Rosemary started to beg him to marry her. She was on her knees at the end, sobbing as Howard kept trying to get away. I was outraged. I wanted to call out "Forget it, he's not good enough for you!" But again, I remembered to keep silent.

The afternoon continued this way with people sobbing, begging, screaming, attacking, and so on. Literature has taught me that life is indeed filled with these episodes, so I was not surprised. What *did* surprise me, however, is that when they finished, they simply looked calmly at Morgan, nodded at his responses, smiled, sat down, and drank water as if nothing had happened.

And suddenly it was six! We set off for home, taking a slight detour to pick up two orders of Pad Thai. I settled gratefully into an overstuffed easy chair while Morgan decanted a brisk chardonnay from Argentina. "So, pal, what did you think about today?"

"Oh, Morgan, those poor people! Can you help them, do you think?"

Morgan smiled. "Yes. Yes, I think I helped them today."

"Really? Oh well, you would know, of course, as this is the first time I've seen them."

"But from what you've seen—"

"From what I've seen, Morgan—and yes, I realize I have only lived the life of the mind and must acquaint myself with the blunt, the serendipity, the mystery, the sharp unfolding that is life, and so on. But from what I've seen, they are in terrible, terrible shape."

"Really?" Morgan poured wine into two wineglasses then leaned against the counter, giving the wine—and myself, for that matter—time to breathe.

"Yes. Oh yes. What difficult lives! How they struggled!"

"Yes?" Morgan leaned forward.

"Yes. In spite of such difficulties, how they—"

"Yes?" Morgan was clearly holding his excitement back.

"How they *fought!*"

"Yes!" He clapped his hands sharply. I jumped. I was frankly mystified.

Mystified by this broad spectrum of life, which could contain Doris, who gained so much pleasure from serving real oatmeal to real customers and the many young people I saw today could derive equal delight from washing a floor with no water in the bucket or believing the plastic pitcher with the taped handle was a precious Ming Dynasty vase.

"You see, Nathan, those people today were acting."

"Acting?"

"Yes. They are actors. Meaning that they act."

I hoped there was a further explanation—for don't we all act? Wasn't going to breakfast an action? Wasn't reading *Of Human Bondage* or sewing on a button eye an action?

"Yes. But in the actor's world, these things are all imaginary."

"By *imaginary* you mean . . . none of it is real?"

"That's correct. Like Rip Van Winkle."

"So that man doesn't really carry a revolver."

"Not at all."

"And that woman wasn't really begging that man to confide in her?"

"No. But she very much wants to join the Houston Shakespeare Company and play the *part* of a woman who begs her husband to confide in her."

"Does he?"

"No."

"What happens?"

"He is killed, and then she kills herself."

"I see." I took a quick sip of the chardonnay. "And that lovely young man's wife wasn't really an Olympic swimmer who died?"

"No. In reality, he has no wife. But in reality, he is also an actor who would like to play the part of a man who had a wife who had been an Olympic swimmer, and who had died."

I thought quietly for a moment. "Why?" I finally asked.

"Why?" echoed Morgan thoughtfully.

"Yes. Why would *anyone* want to pretend such a thing?"

"Well, first let me ask you this, Nathan. Did any of them entertain you?"

"Well." I thought carefully. "Does the word continue to mean what its derivation would suggest—that is 'to hold between'?"

"Yes," Morgan said, smiling. "What do you think of the chardonnay?"

"Fulsome, bold and satisfying," I said automatically, my mind wondering what had been held between, and between whom it had been held. "So what was held between the actors and myself was . . . a fiction?"

"Yes."

I munched on a Wheat Thin as we relaxed into the early evening. The light filtering into the parlor now turned everything into a warm sepia print. I felt a deep sense of peace and the miraculous all at once.

"Well then, yes. They did. For at times, I was no longer aware of sitting in a beguiling little room designed by Sanford White, but was actually *with* the young man trying on pants in the fitting room, weeping because he was so fat. And I actually felt I was on a boat with those two young lovers."

"So you believed they were actually young lovers as well?"

"You mean they weren't?" I was shocked. I was ready to concede that the boat was imaginary, but their *ardor*?

"They were just assigned the scene two weeks ago."

"Two weeks? And yet filled with such longing, such hope, such passion for each other?"

"Yes, Nathan. All pretend. All imaginary."

"But I almost called out 'Take the ring! Take the ring!'" I shivered now at how close I had come to humiliating myself.

"But did you not also—and I do not mean to pry—but did you perhaps find yourself reflecting on your own hopes, dreams, ardor, longing, and passion as well?"

I suddenly remembered Doris and my idea about the Circle Line cruise. Once again, I blushed deeply and was thankful for the dim sepia-toned light.

"Yes I did, Morgan."

"Well then, even better."

"What a strange thing the theater is. I must say that until last night, when I perused *Our Town*, I had read no plays. Nor had I ever *seen* a play, for the Patterson household did not acknowledge the theater."

"But you and Emma Louise participated deeply in the theatrical experience."

"We did?" I asked, dumbfounded.

"Did you not believe, those times you hid behind the couch, that indeed you *were* secret agents?"

"Oh! Oh my, yes! We both *absolutely* believed when Mrs. Carmichael asked for another gin and tonic that she meant it was safe for the boats to land this evening. And that if we didn't get our message through, the entire Free World was doomed to perdition."

I was astonished at recalling how Emma and I had held our respective breaths, how we had crept away stealthily to the upstairs study where—using a large stapler as our rudimentary telegraph—we communicated the information in Morse code to our comrades.

"Why?" asked Morgan.

"Why what?" I asked.

"Why would *anyone* want to pretend such a thing?" Morgan asked, smiling.

"Oh! Because . . . because . . ." I thought long and hard. "Because it was so much *fun.*"

"Exactly," said Morgan. "And *that's* why we call them 'plays'."

I took another sip of the excellent chardonnay, astonished as always by how words often came around to meaning exactly what they claimed to mean.

"Both you and Emma Louise understood what Aristotle told us: theater is instinctual."

"My goodness! To have rubbed shoulders with *Aristotle* as we sat quietly behind the couch!"

"I'm going to get tickets for the heiress, what do you say?" asked Morgan.

"Sure, Morgan," I answered, not sure what doing a favor for a potentially rich woman had to do with our discussion.

It might have been the flood of memories which had come back to me today, or the fact that they had come back with an import worthy of Aristotle's *Poetics*, but I was frankly thankful that the rest of the evening could be spent with a small tray of Pad Thai as we watched the New Orleans Saints battle the New York Giants.

The Heiress

Rich burgundy velvet seats and carpeting met us as we entered the theater. An elderly maid dressed in black with a doily about her neck showed us to our seats. I gazed upward at the beautiful ceiling and walls, the sconces, the chandelier. There was general atmosphere of warmth and volubility. I might add that the two of us looked particularly dashing—Morgan wearing a navy velvet jacket and I with a white silk scarf. I had worried about being overdressed, but Morgan assured me that this was New York. I was beginning to realize that saying "This is New York" serves to remind us that anything is not only possible, but thoroughly acceptable.

I paged through my playbill, admiring the few pictures and especially enjoying the descriptions of various restaurants. Morgan explained that each actor had a small paragraph describing what else they had done. I eagerly read through but was surprised at how little everyone had done.

"How *little?*" Morgan asked.

"Why yes, Morgan. We could fill up a paragraph just describing what we do in one day! Today for instance: pancakes at the Studio Coffee Shop, visiting Bed Bath and Beyond, buying books and candy bars to bring to Marsha who is in the hospital for a double knee replacement, a brief discussion on the nature of existentialism over a supper of pasta with anchovies and sun-dried tomatoes, now the theater, perhaps ending our evening with some tiramisu." (The latter was added in a hopeful tone of voice.)

Morgan started to speak, but my attention was diverted when I realized my vision was failing terribly.

"Morgan, I think I may be going blind!" I whispered, terrified.

"Hang on, pal," Morgan said soothingly. "The show is starting."

I was grateful to see that, sure enough, as the lights came down— *house lights*, I was later to learn—the curtain went up. And, dear reader, from that moment until the end, I was lost, unaware of my rich burgundy velvet seat, my silk scarf, my playbill, even my breathing.

For a more painful situation cannot be conceived: a sweet and darling woman who believed so dreadfully that she could only be loved for her pending inheritance alone! Oh, dastardly father who planted such an ugly seed of doubt into the heart of a woman whose soul and heart and mind were beautiful, and who—when she changed out of those dreadful orange plaid gowns into that delightful confection of white lace and organdy—became outwardly so beautiful that I, like so many in the audience, experienced a sharp intake of breath.

But too late! Too late, for now the actions of the suitor matched so perfectly what the father presaged—that the young woman could never believe herself to be beautiful, to be worthy of a young man's love! But *were* they the actions of a rapacious and villainous fortune seeker, or did they only *seem* so because the father had planted that seed? And was not happiness possible even if he *had* been merely a fortune hunter? For he was tall and strong and good-looking, and if you love even a very bad man fiercely and passionately, is that love not worth something? Does that love not provide a future far better than the final legacy with which that poor woman was left, owing to the dark seed planted by her father?

As she ascended that staircase and her suitor pounded on that front door which was to be forever bolted, I wanted to cry "Let him in! Let him in!" But alas, the curtain fell slowly, as if sealing her life up forever. I was shattered. I was shaken. Was it that I myself felt a hearkening back to my own distant past when I wanted to say to Elvira, "Take him back! Take him back! With all his faults and all that pains you, take back the love that started on Walnut and Main and run away to the wilds of Florida, where you might still be paddling!"

But before I could become conscious of this magical intermingling between the shattered woman climbing the stairs and my memories of Elvira, the curtain was up again and everyone was walking toward us and bowing and the audience so docile, so still that no one had seemed even to breathe over those three hours had now erupted into ferocious applause and there were shouts and cries!

And how delighted I was to see that sweet girl present a deep curtsey, holding hands with both her father *and* her suitor, and *everyone smiling*! And then her father brought her forward gently and she bowed alone, and people were on their feet shouting "Brava! Brava!" And I asked Morgan to please stand so that I could sit on his shoulder and trumpet madly. And so it all ended in a fierce and exuberant celebration, and I realized then and there that it had all been pretend, just as Morgan had said.

"But will I someday *remember* that it is pretend, Morgan? And not experience the deep intermingling that was so personal this evening?" I asked over my tiramisu and decaf cappuccino.

"Not if they do their jobs right, as they did tonight."

"But did *you* forget, Morgan?"

"I did indeed."

This seemed startling to me, not simply because he is my mentor but because he has been in this business for twenty-five years or so.

"But age has nothing to do with it, Nathan. We are all hungry to play again, as we did when children."

And again I remembered Emma Louise and myself and our hushed suspense behind the couch, when our notepad and our stapler were all we had to save the Free World. We believed everything, and it was just as good (but how was that possible?)—just as good as this tiramisu tonight, but in a different way.

The Spin on Eleventh Avenue

It was the first time I had ever actually seen a face "blanche visibly"—although, of course, this is a phrase I have read time and time again, particularly in the detective genre. Particularly when a shaggy but intuitive detective is able to point his finger at the least likely houseguest and accuse her of murder.

With one delicately veined hand, Madeleine dropped her sherry glass while the other equally delicately veined hand lifted itself to her chest to quiet its sudden heave beneath her beaded gown. She rose unsteadily and patted her mousey hair as if to command a presence of mind.

"I-I don't know what to say!" She laughed thinly. "I! I—a *murderess*! I whose only passion is my volunteer work with bonsai plants at the Botanic Gardens! I who loved Jonathan as a brother!"

"NOT merely as a brother, mademoiselle!"

"I—"

"You were his *mistress*!"

41

The occupants of the room inhaled as one—Charles, stodgy beside the mantle; Muffy, plumply sequestered by the candy box; Maxine, alluring and off-putting, cigarette lighter in one hand; Reggie unaccountably holding a tennis racquet even as he was dressed in black tie for dinner. All the siblings, for the first time in their lives, united in that one incredulous gasp.

"And when he chose instead *this* woman," Monsieur Chevaux gestured to the alluring yet off-putting Maxine, "you killed him. The evidence is incontrovertible. For he had been *raked* to death—a very tiny rake, the only purpose for which would be to tend a bonsai plant. An original weapon, made more gruesome by its itsy-bitsy nature!"

Madeleine's face blanched visibly.

But it is not the details of a fictional mind-set wherein we dwell, dear reader, but an actual September morning, clear and brilliant. Today, on our way to breakfast, I asked Morgan to stop at a "previously owned" car dealership. I was now gesturing to a Ford Taurus, blue with white interior, and Morgan's face had blanched visibly.

"But-but what are you suggesting, Nathan?"

"That we buy this car and take a few day trips here and there."

"But . . . but who would drive?"

"I can't, Morgan," I said patiently. "I don't have a license."

"Then who?"

"Morgan. *You* have a driver's license."

"Yes. So?"

I smiled at his deliberate obtuseness and said to Moe, a kind man in a brilliant plaid jacket with wide lapels, that we needed a minute to confer. He graciously sidled away, lighting up a cigar over a cup of joe.

"I'm not a very good driver, Nathan," said Morgan, settling into a lovely bright red dinette chair that had been courteously placed by a coffee machine whose numerous buttons provided coffee in every combination of sugar and milk imaginable.

"I'm not picky." I shrugged, looking longingly at the coffee machine, realizing too late that I should have waited on my impulse until after breakfast.

"But *why*, Nathan? Surely there are so many wonderful corners of New York you would like to explore—easily arrived at by subway, bus, or taxi."

"Of course, Morgan. But brilliant autumn days are going to start whispering 'Foliage tour! Foliage tour!' And there will be no better place to answer the call than New England," I said knowingly, for indeed images of Connecticut with its vast spectrum of autumnal hues were as fresh in my memory as if jumping into piles of leaves and drinking cider happened just yesterday.

"Foliage—"

"Tour," I finished helpfully.

"A foliage tour?!" Morgan's voice popped into its high register, causing Moe to look over at us questioningly. I waved my trunk at him happily, indicating everything was fine.

Morgan, elbows on his knees, placed his head in his hands. "Shall I get us some coffee, Morgan?" I asked hopefully.

"Yes. Extra sugar and cream for me, please."

I trotted up to the machine and got both of us coffee with extra sugar and cream, marveling that a machine could take such specific requests. I was also pleased to find yet another machine that offered numerous pastries and chose two cheese Danishes, marveling again at both the serendipity and generosity of life.

I settled our meal on a small table that had been thoughtfully provided for just such an occasion and, over the steaming cup of coffee and fresh Danish, once again gave thanks for capitalism.

"For *capitalism?*" asked Morgan, gratefully latching on to a subject that had nothing to do with driving.

"Perhaps this is a simplistic way of acknowledging such an enormous concept whose roots go far deeper than mere economic theory," I said, taking a large bite of my cheese Danish. "Nonetheless, I am most happy to spend a few coins and keep the Coffee-O-Matic Company rich if it means I in turn am supplied with easy and serendipitous comfort. Is not this coffee machine, with the immediate adventure it supplies, a microcosmic version of the impetus behind westward expansion, for instance?"

Morgan raised his eyebrows as he is wont to do when a new or interesting thought comes his way and then proceeded to unwrap his Danish. We ate and drank in companionable silence. When our cups and cellophane wrappers were empty, the silence continued for a moment, and I waited hopefully, expectantly.

"I suppose we could at least *sit* in one," Morgan murmured.

"Moe! Moe!" I gestured to the sweet and stocky gentleman who then hurried to us, lapels and cuffs flapping in the breeze. "We are ready to sit in one!"

"Great! Great!" And he hustled, I trotted, and Morgan warily approached the '89 Ford Taurus.

"Front wheel drive, disc brakes, air bags, speed control, automatic windshield wipers, air-conditioning."

"Oh my heavens!" I breathed, astonished. "Is this a *radio?*"

Morgan looked at me a bit witheringly.

"Why yes, little fellah," said Mo genially. "And it will play all your rock-and-roll favorites!"

"All my rock-and-roll favorites!" I said happily, not at all certain what they were. "Oh, Morgan! Shall we take this baby out for a spin?"

"A *spin!*" Morgan's voice once more slipped into a higher register.

"Only way you can be sure of its easy, smooth road handling, Mr. Johansson." And once again, I found myself being seated on a huge stack of NYNEX phone books.

"Thank you, Moe," I said happily, marveling once again at how often these generous New Yorkers feel responsible for our optical enjoyment.

"Not at all, little fellah," he whispered, gently rebuckling my seat belt. "Frankly, I see you are the motivating factor here, if you catch my meaning. What I mean to say is, Mr. Johansson seems like a nice guy and all, but perhaps he's a poet or something, am I right?"

"He works in the theater," I said.

"That's what I thought. Fact is, artists generally need guidance in worldly matters."

"Uh-huh." I listened raptly for all points of view are a point of fascination with me. And frankly, I was still mesmerized by those lapels.

"I don't suppose you have an inside track here somewhere, for those of us who haven't driven in a while?" Morgan asked hopefully.

Moe smiled at me to indicate his point was well illustrated. "No, sir. But Eleventh Avenue should be no problem today."

"The Eleventh Avenue located in *New York City*, sir?" Morgan's voice was, for him, heavily laced with irony, but not heavily enough for Moe.

"The very same. Go on with you now," Moe added generously, but Morgan seemed paralyzed.

"Morgan," I said softly, "perhaps you also need to allow into your life the bluntness, the serendipity, the mystery, the sharp unfolding that is life."

While admittedly clothed in a lush array of literate syntax, the above still registered as a gauntlet thrown down; and within moments, Morgan had turned on the car, lurched us into and out of forward and backward several times, and finally put it in reverse. While such an initial foray was a bit jolting, it was good to note that the brakes and seat belts were in fine condition. Morgan backed us eloquently onto Eleventh Avenue, and after pausing briefly in first and second gears, he thrust us thoroughly into drive and we were suddenly accelerated into the rich autumnal day, accompanied by windshield fluid spurting, wipers wiping, headlights blinking, and a general series of syncopated honks.

Gentle reader, I am determined not to become that tiresome sort of narrator who uses each and every miracle of the present to expostulate on an aspect of his past; however, may I say that this ride—which would have been exhilarating simply from Morgan's unique methodology—was made even more so by the fact that I had never moved at any pace faster than Morgan's own stride which, brisk as it was, never allowed my ears to flap gently in the wind.

For I need not elaborate on the fact that being wedged in a dark crate with magazines, material scraps, and children's blocks, transported from Bristol to New York, and then seeing the light of day while lying on a flea market table, can at best be compared to the effects of anesthesia. But to be poised on a pile of NYNEX phone books with the wind shouting through an open window is to be nothing less than master and commander of one's fate, with the Ford Taurus a great ship and the open road one great ocean of possibility.

Lumberjack Specials

We are seated in our booth at the Studio Coffee Shoppe, where happily for us, "Breakfast is served all day!" The sunlight cascades over the dusty green plants in the front window and highlights the mottled pate of Mr. Turnip Head, who awaits his next delivery. I nod to him happily, and he waves back, smiling, revealing two gold teeth. We sip our coffee, and Morgan stares moodily at the rim of his cup.

"But you did very well, Morgan."

"VERY WELL?"

"We're alive, aren't we?"

"Yes."

"That's more than can be said for a great many people." I gazed happily through the front windows, and instead of the hustle and bustle of Eighth Avenue, I see our morning's adventures. "Wasn't the tunnel wonderful? And then all those large roads? And trucks? And oil tanks? And that delightful little rest area with the postcards? And that nice policeman."

"Nice?"

"Well, in a hearty, rough-cut kind of way."

"His face looked like a side of beef!"

"Well, yes," I agreed, not certain how that mattered, but then remembered my own fastidious judgment of elephants fashioned from satin and lace overlay.

"It was the end of the month, so he probably had a quota of tickets he had to pass out."

"But, Morgan, you didn't get a ticket."

"True, but his finger was itching. I could see it. You probably couldn't see it."

"I thought it was very kind of him to encourage you."

"Encourage me?"

"Well, yes. Now I don't know much about the complexities of being in the driver's seat. However, it seems to me when driving on the New Jersey Turnpike, we should be moving faster than a dog with three legs, as they say."

Doris arrived with our lumberjack specials: "two eggs done any way you like 'em, pancakes or french toast, bacon, ham or sausage, chilled juice and our unending pot of piping-hot pure Columbian Coffee!!" She refilled our cups and gave me a wink. I shivered and watched her lovely plumpness recede behind the counter. Morgan suddenly laughed, all moodiness gone in a moment. I looked at him in surprise.

"You remind me of someone, pal."

"Who?" I asked, taking a bite of perfectly cooked bacon.

"Me."

Let me say, reader, that this is high praise indeed for I must confess now that, whether it is the many years I kept shoulder with the great masters from St. Augustine to Thomas Merton, Mallory to Jack Higgins, Edgar Allan Poe to Dorothy Sayers, Homer to . . . to . . .

"James Joyce?"

"Oh lord. No, Morgan. Remember I lived in Bristol, Connecticut."

Morgan nodded thoughtfully and took a bite of french toast.

And the recent relationship I have made with the computer, I have a sudden and splendid passion: to become a writer. And if I reminded this superbly literate gentleman of *himself*, then I had a leg up, as they say.

"To *become* a writer."

"Yes, Morgan," I said excitedly.

"And what exactly have you been doing all this time?"

"All this time?"

"Yes. What do all these pages all have in common?" He paused. "Take your time."

"Well. I suppose . . . I suppose what you're getting at is that . . . is that I have *been* writing."

"Yes, Nathan."

"Odd. That never actually occurred to me."

"To *call* it writing, you mean."

"Yes. Exactly."

"Well, I'm not surprised."

"You're not?"

"No. I think you have achieved a state of grace."

"A state of grace?" I asked, awed at the very idea, my breakfast forgotten—indeed, my forkful of egg frozen in midair.

"Yes. Because a state of grace is when distinction vanishes. And when distinction vanishes, the need to call a thing by a name—for instance, to call a thing 'writing'—vanishes as well. It's a tremendous thing, really. One might say moving backwards in the development of language, of concept."

"Moving backwards," I said. "Like Merlin, getting younger."

"Very much so. My point is that, for you, writing has become a bit like breathing."

"You mean of a sort of involuntary nature."

"Exactly."

"But, Morgan, why then do we have a word for breathing?"

Morgan paused to consider, his forkful of egg now frozen in midair.

"Perhaps the word 'breathing' needed to be invented after someone had *stopped* breathing," he mused.

"Oh?" I asked cagily, opening a butter packet. For in truth, I wasn't always certain when Morgan was *investigating* a concept or *playing* with it.

"Well, when a person died for the first time, the second person said—and there must have been a third person as well, come to think of it, so the second person could say, 'Look! Fred is not . . . is not . . . is not . . . 'You see, they had no word for it. And the third person said, 'Is not—is not what?' And the second person said—"

"Well, the second person could have said 'His chest is not going up and down.'" Doris had been serving a businessman nearby and had become engaged by our conversation. She sat down next to me, somewhat enraptured by her own musings.

I choked slightly on my juice and then assumed what I hoped was an air of nonchalance in spite of the napkin I had thoughtlessly tied about my neck.

"No. No, that couldn't be right because it would have meant they had words for 'chest,' 'up,' and 'down.' Never mind," she said, embarrassed at having insinuated herself into the conversation and beginning to leave our booth.

"Oh, but I'm sure they did!" I said, more to keep her sitting with us than actually thinking how that could be.

"Really?" said Doris. "But how could that be?"

I was stymied.

"Well, here's how," offered Morgan. "Perhaps Fred's wife, Gladys, had reason so say during their short time together, 'Let me measure your *chest* for a new tiger skin garment. Please put *down* the club for a moment and lift *up* the baby mammoth while I sweep.' And so on."

"Of course. So when they first saw the distinction between an aliveness, a chest going up and down and not going up and down, they decided. 'We better call this something.'"

I was still not convinced. "But you are saying the negative, 'not breathing,' gave birth to the state that preceded the negative. That is, 'breathing.'"

"I might be," said Morgan. "For out of chaos comes order. Out of darkness, light. Out of silence, The Word."

I had to credit Morgan with his reasoning, having spent years poring over the family Bible, marveling at its poetry and magnitude of thought.

"Oh, that is so exciting," said Doris. "Really. I sometimes find myself wondering where all the words came from and why we aren't making any more. Oh, I know. *Quark* and *photon* and *telemarketing* and so on. But really, how often do you need those? Does it mean all the really important things like *flour* and *home* and *gardening* and *bubble baths*—"

"*Dawn, velvet, sensuality*—" added Morgan.

"*Wind, sepia-toned light, gardenia*," I said (the last tremulously, for it was indeed the very scent that Doris had brought with her into our cozy booth).

"*Uppercut, T-bone, cigar, womenfolk*," offered Mr. Turnip Head.

"*Forensic, viewpoint, rigmarole*," called the gentleman nearby, looking over his *New York Times*.

"Oh, wouldn't it have been wonderful to be the first person to name a thing—to say, 'We and all future generations shall call that a *napkin dispenser*!' Although, of course, it wouldn't have been English, would it?" asked Doris.

"No, but it could easily have been *mappa dispensus*," I said suavely, casually stepping on my napkin and letting it fall silently to the floor.

"*Mappa dispensus*," she said, enjoying each syllable.

As one we sat silently together, lingering over our chosen words and concepts, wondering if—in our lives—we would find a thing to name.

"Oh! But we mustn't forget the whole point was that you've achieved a state of grace!" Doris shook herself back to the present. "I congratulate you. I do!"

Mr. Turnip Head nodded, and the businessman raised his cup in a toast. Doris poured us more coffee and was on her way before I had time to recover from her sudden proximity, her sweet scent.

"Gardenia," I said to Morgan.

"I know where we can get her some if you like."

"Oh, Morgan, it is so forward! To say 'I'll have two eggs over easy, home fries, and whole wheat toast and—oh, by the way, here's some gardenia cologne I just thought you might enjoy!' Oh, I just *couldn't!*" I was horrified at the thought.

"Then we'll find out when her birthday is. For certainly, a birthday allows for a gift that can range from simple thoughtfulness to a more meaningful connotation."

"Oh!" I felt lightheaded. What with Doris's sudden proximity, three cups of coffee, the gentle scent of gardenia, the bright sunlight, and the morning's exhilarating discovery of tunnels and oil tanks, I suddenly felt that if a state of grace allows for a vanishing, a return to a oneness, then today I was very much aware of a thrilling distinction, a thing outside myself. And if I could have been the first to name it, I would have called it *bliss.*

Balancing at the Cloisters

Be assured, reader, that each day brings new and serendipitous experiences to this old elephant's life, be it nearly tumbling off my chair as an actor pierces my heart with his struggle, newly abutted taste sensations such as fried tofu wedges smothered in a spicy peanut sauce, whisking through the Lincoln Tunnel (for indeed, Morgan is inching toward a personal record of forty miles per hour), or going to the theater—not only to the gloriously opulent Broadway houses but in all sorts of dark and tiny spaces where young actors with a few folding chairs and oddly painted bureaus act beneath lights made out of large paint cans.

"Morgan," I whispered during an intermission one evening in just such a tiny theater as I have described, as we sipped apple juice and ate chocolate chip cookies, "I think I like some of these plays better."

"Better than what, pal?" Morgan whispered back.

"Better than some things we have seen in the gloriously opulent Broadway houses."

"Uh-huh." Morgan nodded as if this made perfect sense.

"But why is that?" I asked as we scurried back for the third act of Shaw's *Arms and the Man*, pressed in a sweet tumult of our fellow audience members.

"Because they often *are* better," he said, as always illuminating what seems a dark and impenetrable mystery with the bright light of fact. And as the lights came down, we returned to the delightful adventures of the Chocolate Soldier.

But one of my especially serendipitous discoveries was what must certainly be the pride of every Manhattanite: the subway.

"I'm wondering," Morgan said politely into the tiny microphone in the Plexiglas window, "if I need a token for my friend here."

"Elephants ride free," the tired dark-skinned gentleman said.

"Thank you very much," Morgan said, and we pressed through the turnstile together.

When that noisy tubular conveyance whisked its way into the station, I had a glorious uplift of affectionate reverence at such technology, similar perhaps to what dear Emily Dickinson felt when she wrote: "I like to see it lap the miles and lick the valleys up." And I wondered suddenly if an affectionate reverence was a key to good writing, a key that might allow my work to reach beyond its feeble attempts thus far at the genres of romance and the cozy detective novel.

We squished ourselves into a seat between two fat people with equally obese shopping bags, the subway doors closed smoothly, and we were off, stopping at Thirty-Fourth Street where hundreds of people pressed their way in, at Forty-Second where those hundred exchanged themselves for a new and equally boisterous batch, and then at Fifty-Ninth when a good many left and we were able to breathe more fully again.

But then such glorious and unexpected velocity! We did not stop until we reached 125th Street! At one point, I gave a heartfelt "Wheee!" causing one tired woman to look up from her paperback.

"First time?" she asked.

"Yes."

"That's sweet."

"I suppose," I said, now embarrassed about my sheltered life.

"But I still love it too," Morgan said. "And I've done this for twenty years. I suppose it never wears off for some of us."

"Yeah," the woman nodded, returning to her paperback.

I once again gave thanks to Destiny for placing me in this ageless gentleman's hands, for we all will be given a first time, but only those who are vigilant and who proceed with affectionate reverence will return to that first time again and again.

Almost as if my ruminations on vigilance and affectionate reverence were foreordained, when we emerged from the cavernous depths of the subway at 190th Street, we were greeted by a sweet forest with leaves beginning to change and the crisp smell of autumn in the air. I gave a sudden gasp for I had forgotten the profound joy autumn brought, the sudden sharp briskness of the air, how the sky seemed more crisply blue than it did at summer. I suddenly remembered being cradled by Emma Louise as the two of us jumped into huge piles of leaves that Emmet raked. I gave a sigh and then crouched deeper into Morgan's pocket. The two of us gazed long at the lovely beauty, and as we made our way along the path, our ears were met with "Christus factus est pro nobis," a profoundly sweet Gregorian chant.

"Close your eyes, Morgan!" I commanded.

He did so.

I paused. "Now, can you not imagine yourself at the cloister of the Monasterio de Santo Domingo de Silos?"

"I can," said Morgan. "But then I think I was once a monk," Morgan offered in what I would consider to be an exceedingly offhanded way, given the content of his sentence.

"Really? You mean . . . many years ago, and then you were perhaps a victim of amnesia and-and—"

"No."

"From a fishing accident, or no! Of course, while climbing Craig Patrick, in a storm—"

"Nathan."

"Alone, while carrying an offering at night, your sandals slipped and—"

"Nathan! Hush now!" I hushed. Morgan continued, "I meant in a previous life."

"A previous life!" I breathed the concept with as much amazement and tender awe as I had yesterday's notion of a state of grace. That life could be so full as all this and yet happen again!

"Oh, Morgan, I see it all so clearly! You fell in love with a young nun. A novitiate. Your eyes met one day over the communion rail. You tried to ignore it, the deep and profound sense all at once of love and loss—"

"Nathan."

"For you were both married already to your Lord. You try to continue as before, Sister Theresa tending her garden, you your pharmacy. But still the passion, the sense of oneness, of coming home. *This love out of time* simply could not be denied—"

"Nathan, quiet now. People are beginning to—"

"And so, one morning, you and Sister Theresa hurry away. All you have are your simple robes, sandals, rosary beads, three small turnips, and a bouquet of wild sage. You set sail for Bordeaux, crossing the treacherous Bay of Biscay. A storm arises. Sister Theresa—who has now reverted to her former name, Felicia Marisa Alyssa—topples overboard. You reach out, she is gone. You arrive at Bordeaux a broken man and set up a small shop where you make small religious articles out of birch. Years pass. You stay true to your Felicia Marisa Alyssa even though the women of France are *très charmante*. And then one day, one late autumnal afternoon much like this one, you look up from your tiny lathe to see a sweet gentle face peering into your window, her eye having been caught by a small crèche scene done in the style of the craftsman of Barcelona. She wanders in. *Is* it? Could it *be*? Do your eyes (now grown weary from working so late at night crafting small religious articles) deceive you? And she says one word, one word only, for these many years she has been unable to speak. She says—"

"Yes?" Morgan asked, settling comfortably on a stone wall, knowing it was merely a matter of time before my torrent of prose would run out.

"Uh . . ." I was stymied. "She says . . ." But I was at a loss. "She says . . ."

"Rosebud," offered a young woman, who had sat listening unbeknownst to us.

We turned to her.

"Because of a movie you both loved," she added for my benefit as Morgan had begun to chuckle in a knowing way.

"A *movie?*" I asked, uncertainly, wondering if she had missed the clear references to the medieval time period.

As if reading my mind, she said, "Because, as you said yourself, it was a love out of time."

"Ah," I said, feeling suddenly moved by the possibility. What else could *a love out of time* portend than that a previous life could be affected by a future one?

"Thank you so much," said Morgan.

"Oh, you are very welcome." She smiled and wandered down a lovely Romanesque hall, probably from the Poitou region, circa 1152 or thereabouts.

"Really? You know that just by looking?" asked Morgan, amazed, although his attention seemed far more riveted by the young woman's gently receding back than by the lovely pair of portal lions, probably Northern Italian, most definitely of the early thirteenth century.

"Well, yes, I think so," I said, my mind only vaguely on issues of provenance, still riveted as *I* was from the notion of the intermingling of time past and present. "Certainly no later than 1180."

"You're serious then."

"Well, yes," I said, confused, as I could construe no humorous or comic tone to the information.

"But how?"

"Morgan," I said patiently, "I am certain that you, as well as all our readers, are tired of these continual references to the reading I did for thirty years or so."

"But still—"

"But of all the materials I had at my disposal, I suppose my favorite were the stacks on medieval literature and art."

"Stacks?"

"Stacks, Morgan. Stacks and stacks."

Morgan had stopped suddenly. I felt the reaction a bit strong for such simple information.

"Why?"

"Why what?"

"Why stacks?"

"Why not?"

"Well, the way you describe them, the gentleman with the stubborn jaw who had hit his head too long upon his cradle—"

"Grampy Patterson."

"And his taciturn wife with the gentle blue eyes—"

"Grammy Patterson."

"And your lovely creator with the delicate white hands—"

"Dear Elvira."

"And the gentleman who was last seen paddling a canoe of his own making—"

"Emmet Haines."

"None of them sound particularly like a medievalist."

"But *someone* was, Morgan," I said.

He nodded. "It's a clue. To what, I don't know."

As I trotted along behind Morgan through the aforementioned Romanesque hall, I mused on the miracle of a clue. Like the tiny toylike bonsai rake! Could it be I was writing my way into my own future? How, I wondered, would it turn out?

"I wonder how much it would be for my friend," Morgan asked the delicate woman at the admissions desk.

"Elephants are free on Tuesdays," she said, patting my head gently and fitting the little tin button on my ear. "Is that okay?" she asked.

I nodded happily and received another pat for my seeming good nature, when in fact a small tin button is nothing compared to a toddler's first set of bicuspids.

Morgan abruptly steered us away from a tour which had just begun in the Fuentiduena Chapel, as he has a strong aversion to being part of a group, especially one being told to look at something. We arrived at the lovely doors of the Moutiers-Saint-Jean monastery flanked by two kings standing free in their canopied niches.

"They look happy to see us," mused Morgan. "They seem to be checking our names off a large and gracious guest list."

"Actually, it is thought that these figures represent Clovis, the first Christian ruler of France, and his son Clothar. In the year of his conversion, probably around 496, Clovis granted this monastery a charter that exempted it in perpetuity from both royal and ecclesiastical jurisdictions. These long pieces of papers, or banderoles, may in fact represent the charter of 496."

"Really?" said Morgan, as always respectful of new information, and in this instance, perhaps even more enraptured as it came from a toy elephant.

"Indeed. But I think your interpretation far exceeds these dry facts and more becomes a place of worship." And we waved genially to the gentlemen as we passed and into the warm loving light of the Langdon Chapel.

"This could actually make a believer out of me," Morgan said quietly. And we both sat on the tiny wooden chairs and gazed at the lovely enthroned Virgin and Child—probably from Burgundy, about 1130, carved from a single block of birch with traces of paint still visible—for quite some time, the afternoon sun casting shafts of light through the three lovely windows in the tabernacle.

We proceeded gently into the St. Guilhelm Cloister, slowly walking its perimeter, marveling at the beautifully carved capitals, admiring the lovely grasses, the daffodils, and sweet William.

We made our way carefully through the treasury, giving every article genuine consideration, although I must admit I favored the rosary bead no larger than a golf ball which, when opened, revealed numerous biblical scenes, all finely detailed, with horses and camels and houses and churches and people and kings and saints. In my fascination, I felt suddenly as if I could be subsumed into the busy, boisterous scenes crafted so finely from boxwood and was grateful when Morgan picked me up and moved me on.

"We wonder at choosing a monastic life, however, in comparison to the harshness of secular life of those early centuries, this was an excellent choice, especially if you were poor," I mused. "A life of thought, of prayer, of mediation with its rigorous responsibilities, to be sure, and its denials—but still a life of purity in so many ways."

"Yes," agreed Morgan quietly.

"But not for everyone," I added quickly, hoping I hadn't reminded him of that painful time when he forsook the priesthood for Sister Theresa.

"No, not for everyone."

Morgan seemed oddly thoughtful, perhaps owing to the atmosphere of the Cloisters. I myself—while grateful for the peace and calm which arose so naturally from such a place of beauty, for the sweet integrity of line and form, the extraordinary craftsmanship of the Unicorn Tapestries and the twelfth-century walrus-ivory cross from the abbey at Bury St. Edmunds—was now quite happily entranced by an excellent brie and sun-dried tomato sandwich on whole-grain toast with fruit garnish in a nearby cafe. Morgan had finished his egg salad sandwich and was now concentrating on balancing backward on his chair, its front legs up, allowing his feet to dangle freely. His arms were crossed, and he gazed straight ahead, lost perhaps in the possibilities of love lost and then regained in a small wood carving shop in Bordeaux, some six hundred years ago.

The cafe was empty save for one other customer, who coincidentally happened to be the young woman who had so aptly finished my short synopsis earlier in the day. She had not noticed us, being rather fairly taken by her book on the War of the Roses, and I wondered if this was perhaps the true source of Morgan's thoughtfulness.

"Morgan?" I asked, but he did not seem to hear. "Morgan!"

"Yes?" He jumped, almost losing his balance but regaining it quickly.

"Why don't you ask her to join us?"

"I couldn't!" he said, abashed.

"Too forward?" I wondered.

"Far, far too forward," he agreed.

"Then we should find out her birthday," I suggested.

"We should *what?*" But then he realized that once again the mantle of action had been returned to him. "Couldn't you on one or two occasions forget something, Nathan?" he asked.

"Probably not." I shrugged. "Are you going to eat your pickle?"

The young woman got up to get more coffee.

"Oh, hello!" she called out happily. "Isn't this a wonderful place?"

"Oh yes, it is!" I answered when it seemed Morgan had something caught in his throat.

"Have you tried their carrot cake?"

"No, I haven't. This is my first time, actually. My name is Nathan, and this is Morgan."

"How do you do?" she said. "My name is Abby."

"Abby? What an excellent name!"

"Oh no, not really."

"Really. Isn't Abby a fine name, Morgan?"

"Yes," Morgan said, looking at his shoes.

"And particularly apt for a visit to the Cloisters," I added, then wished I hadn't for it could be a confusing comment. But Abby immediately responded with a generous and warm laugh as she refilled her cup.

"Are you interested in the War of the Roses?" I called to her.

"Oh, very much so. Are you?"

"Well, actually, I am interested in just about everything."

"Really? Good for you."

We seemed to have exhausted the conversational gambits of strangers, for Morgan suddenly seemed entranced with tying and retying his shoes.

With a smile, Abby suddenly grabbed a napkin and wrote something down, carefully folding the napkin in half and placing it in her book. Having recently entered into the life of the writer, I understood the need to "get something down as soon as it comes to you." Was it my understanding of her impulse that drove my own impulse which was to shout, "WHEN'S *YOUR* BIRTHDAY, ABBY?"

In retrospect, I will admit, the question was a bit clumsy, a bit out of the blue. Even so, Morgan's sudden toppling backward seemed an overreaction.

"Oh my goodness! Oh my goodness, are you all right?" Abby rushed to Morgan's side, and even as I held my breath and gazed from my safe perch on the marble table, I could see they made a nice pair.

"Oh, I'm fine," Morgan said casually, trying to get up.

"No. No, stay a moment here."

"I—"

"No. Stay!"

Abby's voice carried such sudden authority that Morgan actually lay back down, as if he were a docile golden retriever.

"Sorry. I'm sure you're fine, but still, let's give the body one or two moments to collect itself. 'To find your smile,' as a little boy informed me the other day at the playground."

"To find my smile?" asked Morgan.

"Exactly. He had fallen off the seesaw and immediately took himself over to sit beneath a tree. I ran to him to make sure he was all right, and he said, 'I'm fine, but I have to take a moment and find my smile before I get back on the seesaw.'"

"Brilliant," said Morgan.

"Absolutely brilliant," agreed Abby. "How many times a day should we remind ourselves to stop and not proceed until we find our smile?"

A rather pleasant silence ensued. I looked about, oddly content, and noticed a robin at the window. Suddenly, our sleepy waiter appeared and gazed at the unique tableau.

"Everything okay?" he asked.

"Fine. Morgan? Would you like anything?" I asked.

"Uh . . ." Morgan considered carefully as he gazed upon the timbered ceiling. "I suppose another cup of coffee would be nice."

"And some carrot cake?" I suggested hopefully.

"Will I be able to take solid food soon?" Morgan asked Abby.

"Do you have Jell-O?" Abby asked the waiter.

"No. Sorry."

"Well then, I suppose we can *try* the carrot cake."

"Three pieces," I said to the waiter, for I—for one—had definitely found my smile.

Another pause ensued, which could have been an uncomfortable one but for Abby's sudden realization.

"You know it's interesting, actually, how quickly we gravitate to a chair when we enter a restaurant. Which is understandable, I suppose. However, we completely negate all the angles available to us, all the other ways of gazing upon the world."

Morgan, looking up at the arched ceiling, concurred. "I see what you mean. And really, it's just as easy to come in, lie down on the floor, and order a sandwich, yet no one ever thinks to do this."

Abby joined Morgan on the floor.

"It's like nighttime, isn't it? We negate the world for twelve hours or so. Maybe that has to do with electricity."

"With electricity?" I asked, drawn to this thought in spite of my vow to leave the two of them alone and concentrate on Morgan's coleslaw.

"When you only had a candle, the difference between inside and outside was not all that great," Abby explained.

"I like to watch rooms fade into night," Morgan offered, no doubt remembering the many evenings he and I had spent in sepia-toned light.

"There is a kind of sepia tone to twilight that makes me suddenly think I'm in an old photograph," Abby said.

"Really?" Morgan and I asked together.

"Why, yes!" Abby laughed. "Why?"

But any explanation was cut off by the arrival of the carrot cake and coffee.

"Want yours on the floor?" the waiter asked.

"No, I think we're ready to put the chair back and use it in the traditional fashion. You ready?" Abby asked.

"Wait!" Morgan held up one finger, then smiled. "Yep, looks like I'm ready." And he very nimbly arose from the stone floor and then helped Abby up.

"I come here every month," Abby said, "to be reminded of larger things. It calms me down."

"Are you religious?" I asked between bites of carrot cake.

"No, not formally. Not anymore."

"But you were, once?" I added hopefully, thinking of past lives and wondering if there was even more linkage between Morgan and Abby besides sepia-toned light.

"Nathan!" Morgan warned me quietly, as if once again reading my narrative.

"I was, up to a point. Up to a very impressionable point, but then Confirmation just buried me. I mean, wasn't one of the most refreshing things about Christ the definition of himself through action, through—one might even say—simplicity? Isn't it in the simple actions that we find ourselves having to muster the most courage?"

(I thought of how bringing a small bottle of gardenia cologne to Doris created such a tumult of terror in my soul and realized Abby was quite right.)

Abby continued, "But then don't all these rules and procedures and robes and posturings keep the simple, defining, and courageous moments a bit at a distance?"

"Yes," Morgan said, gazing at her quite intently. "But then aren't they also quite beautiful? And some of us may need beauty. If we are to be redeemed."

When Abby looked up, she met his gaze steadily. I was reminded suddenly of that lovely poem by dear Robert Frost, "Two Look at Two." Although in this case, it was one looking at two, and the one doing that looking was a toy elephant as opposed to two real moose.

"But can we not have beauty without the *Baltimore Catechism*? Or is it that we are simply reminded that everything has a price?" Abby asked, breaking the moment—perhaps because she felt the extraordinary pulse of it, or more likely, because it was an excellent question. She smiled. I could see Morgan was a bit dazzled now and was relieved to see all four legs of his chair were solidly on the ground. There was a lengthy pause. I stilled my fork.

"There you are!" a sharp voice called out from the doorway. "I thought we were meeting at the bookstore!"

"Oh! Jeremy! Is it three thirty already?" Abby was genuinely surprised.

"It's four fifteen! Abby! We have to meet Maxine and Roger at the Top of the Sixes for drinks at five, then we have reservations at Four Seasons for six, and then we have to be at *Morning's at Seven* by eight!"

Had such a sentence ever been uttered? It was a sentence worthy of congratulations, yet Jeremy was fumingly serious, his jaw tense, his body fiercely stiff beneath an excellent navy-blue cashmere overcoat.

"Jeremy, this is Morgan, and this is Nathan," Abby said.

"Pleased to meet you. Let's *go*, Abby." He got out a thin Italian wallet and pulled out two twenties.

"It's fine," Morgan said. "I can take care of this—"

"I can take care of it!" Abby said. "You were injured."

"It's done! Let's go!" Jeremy called over his shoulder as he took the check up to the register.

Morgan stood and suddenly threw down his linen napkin. I tensed.

Abby gathered her coat. She looked at Morgan. There was a pause needing the kind of definition only good writing born of affection could fill.

> The punk had jerked Dollface to him, saying, "Dis' better be da' last time I have to warn you about hanging out with dis' palooka!" Then, throwing down a few crumpled bills, he grabbed his beer and returned to the pool table.
>
> Johansson, Detective for Hire—hating the word *palooka* almost as much as he hated seeing a woman roughly pawed—followed the punk and delivered a perfect uppercut, remembering to lead with his shoulder. The punk was stunned for a moment, then pitched forward onto the marble floor.
>
> Johansson turned to Dollface, who had perched on an oaken table for two, her perfect gams crossed. The late afternoon light cast a rosy shaft across her lithe and womanly body, encased provocatively in a tight green silk dress. Her hair—upswept in a French twist topped by a saucy hat perched at a rakish angle—had been loosened by the punk's roughness, and small tendrils framed her pale and lovely face. She held a cigarette up to her perfect lips, which had been painted in fierce crimson.

"Gotta light, whoever you are?" she asked in a smoky contralto, her hands faintly shaking.

Johansson came toward her in a lithe and soundless fury. He paused, kissed her crimson lips, and set fire to her instead.

"Darling, I'm sorry!" said Jeremy, inappropriately insinuating himself into my narrative. "I get so worried when I can't find you. And tonight is so important."

And Morgan and Abby, far from striding soundlessly or sitting alluringly, merely stood speechlessly. I sighed, noting, not for the first time, the great disparity between art and life.

"Very nice meeting you, Morgan, Nathan. Good-bye." And with a wave, she was gone.

Morgan and I stood for a moment, stunned and bereft. The warm and lovely cafe now seemed cold and lonely. Suddenly tired, we gathered ourselves together and turned at the doorway to bid a good-bye to the room. Suddenly, Morgan sprinted to the table once occupied by Abby.

"Morgan, what is it?" I asked, somewhat mystified and, I admit, still shaken by the knockout punch I had witnessed in my own mind just moments ago.

"She left her book."

"Did she leave her name and address?" I asked, thinking that "Dollface" could be the perfect cover for an espionage agent. And the Cloisters were the perfect place for a "drop," for who would suspect—

"No," Morgan said.

"No?" I asked, a bit downcast.

"But she did leave this. 'Note to self: Love happens in a moment. What happens after that is what happens after that.'"

"Victor Hugo," I nodded.

"Really?" asked Morgan. "I'll have to start reading him."

"You already have," I said.

Morgan smiled and nodded, and soon we were settled on the subway with several other sleepy passengers.

Normally, my curious nature would have had me parsing Abby's meaning, but I was exhausted with the emotions of both the day and the hard-boiled detective genre I had gotten myself into, and so began to doze as a gentleman played the theme song from *The Beverley Hillbillies* on his pocket comb. And the number 2 train lapped the miles to whatever happens after this.

An Unexpected Party Where Things Begin to Happen

The sun was slanting sharply against a lovely marble sculpture of an Aku-Aku, the stalwart guardian of Easter Island, which I had heard tell of in the excellent adventures of Thor Heyerdahl but had heretofore never seen in three dimensions (another great find from a New York City flea market), when Morgan announced that "money was burning a hole in his pocket."

I knew from previous experience that the only way to extinguish the metaphorical conflagration was to buy many new things. So, having written the first draft of "Balancing at the Cloisters," I quickly hit SAVE DOCUMENT and we headed off to a large and imposing store with an infinite diversity of goods that give proof the store feels responsible to all that is beyond bed and bath.

We quickly plucked from the shelves a cookie jar that oinked, an ice cream scoop that mooed, four large teal-colored bath towels with burgundy piping, three giant candles, and two throw rugs for the bath. We tried purified water that tasted as good as what came out of Morgan's tap and some honey-mustard dressing on cucumber slices.

We watched a gentleman demonstrate how to turn apples into peacocks, oranges into dinosaurs, cucumbers into dolphins, and so on. Enraptured, Morgan bought the hardcover instruction book *Zen and the Art of Garnishing* (With Hundreds of Colorful Illustrations) as well as a set of stainless steel sculpting tools ("A $60.00 value. Today: Only $19.95").

Finally we paused, bemused and breathless, before a giant bin of brilliant-colored tropical-fish slippers with safety treads promising warmth, whimsy, and comfort for the incredibly modest price of $10.95.

Just as I began to hope we had earned a stop at the Soap Bar Café with its inviting array of healthy fruit drinks and lemon-poppy seed cakes, Morgan realized the time, hit his head with a characteristic gesture which needs no description here, scooped up four pairs of fish of various colors and species, and steered us briskly through the register and outside where the sidewalk was filled with homeward-bound office workers and the avenue packed with all manner of vehicular items, all headed to the Holland Tunnel with a similar ferocity.

"We've got fifteen minutes to get uptown to a play reading, and at this time and on this corner, it will be absolutely impossible to get a—" Morgan began but miraculously—at *that* very moment and on *that* very corner—a cab pulled up before us. We pushed our way adroitly through the steady stream of pedestrians threatening to surge us southward, but just as we arrived, an elderly woman—portly in a camel-hair coat, hat askew, cane flailing before her as if leading a military charge—collided so vehemently with us that all packages scattered. Fishes flew, the cookie jar oinked, and the ice cream scoop mooed in a chorus of frustration.

"Oh, I am so sorry!" she said above the cacophony. "I'm really so very—"

"No matter!" Morgan managed to keep his composure even as he watched the cab speed away, having been claimed by another fare.

"Oh, and now you've lost the cab! Oh, I am so very sorry! Really! Oh, what a terrible day! Oh, is the store closing!? Oh my! Oh, what will I do for Madeleine's birthday! Oh lord! Watch it, young man!" She now angrily tapped a rather gruesomely pierced bald man with her cane for he had almost stepped on the cow ice-cream scoop. I held my breath, for the man was quite imposing and rather ugly, but he seemed somewhat amazed at the fierceness of this woman and contritely stooped to pick up the scoop, which in turn mooed a thank-you.

"Well, if this isn't the end! You've lost the one cab in New York, I'm due at Madeleine Langwell's birthday party in six minutes, and I haven't a gift!" And I could see for all her fierceness and attention to detail in dress, the effort it took to make her way in a civilized manner while living in New York City was taking its toll. She looked suddenly pale and haggard, propped as she was on her cane and now suddenly near tears.

"Come now," Morgan said, steering her gently and as graciously as possible with two large bags and an elephant in his pocket. "Let's have a cup of tea."

My spirits soared as we entered the warm and cozy restaurant, the windows a bit steamy, the wait staff sleepy, the light warm against the dark.

"This is very kind of you. I don't even particularly *care* for Madeleine Langwell."

Morgan nodded. "I have to admit, we weren't looking forward to the play reading either."

I was wondering if we were only going to have tea or if, in fact, as it was approaching—

"Perhaps we should all order a good meal," Morgan suggested.

"Perhaps," the woman agreed, "as Madeleine is known for chiefly serving canapés. The champagne is always good though. And of course, there will be cake and so on. Yes, I think a meal would be good for us, and that way, we won't be starving and mistakenly breaking open an abstract centerpiece, thinking that the eggs are hard-boiled and finding they are decidedly *not*. Oh, I'm Evelyn Wambaugh."

Morgan and I introduced ourselves and then looked at each other. It seemed as if we were to be included in the party tonight. I was wishing I had brought my silk scarf, for it sounded very upscale, but then how was one to know that a simple trip to buy towels would turn into champagne and brouhaha by the balustrade, as it were?

Fifty minutes later, comfortably full after a meal of pot roast, mashed potatoes, green beans, and apple pie (paid for by Evelyn who insisted, as she was the cause of our having lost our cab), we stood nervously outside apartment 12-A at Gramercy Park West, a pair of fish slippers and *Zen and the Art of Garnishing* wrapped in a *New York Daily News*, having assured Evelyn that such items had been bought for just such an emergency. Even Evelyn seemed a bit nervous. She rang the bell with a gloved finger. We could hear party noises from within. Evelyn suddenly looked up at Morgan.

"Morgan? I wonder if you wouldn't mind if I introduced—"

The door opened. A petite woman dressed in a tiny pearl-gray dress, her face shiny and rapt, her hair so lightly yet fulsomely coifed that it seemed as if a pale gold pile of cotton candy sat upon her head, greeted Evelyn joyously.

"Evelyn! Evelyn darling! How lovely! How wonderful! Oh, I'm so very glad—"

"Madeline! I hope you don't mind, but I brought my son, Morgan."

Morgan—whose face had assumed his official party look (open, genial, bland)—suddenly blanched visibly for the second time in recent memory. His smile became more fixed. It was the kind of smile a corpse would have if a corpse could smile. And I suppose, depending upon the manner of death, a corpse indeed could.

"Your son! But I didn't know you had—"

"And this is Nathan," Evelyn said quickly.

"How charming! It is so very rare to have an elephant here! Please come in! Let me show you where you can put your coats and bags."

She hustled us through numerous guests, through satin and sequins, scarves and lace, suits and wingtips, cheese dips, scents, flutes of champagne; through laughter, high-pitched giggles, nervous undertones; through a whirl of subtle earth tones and large pillows, soft amber lighting, and thick carpeting to her boudoir—a room with a large bed dressed in a subtle Asian duvet barely discernible through the immense pile of coats and hats balanced atop it.

"Come, Evelyn, you must meet Dr. Jermayan. The only reason I could get him away from his practice tonight is that I told him you would be here." She divested Evelyn of her coat, revealing a solid-wool tweed skirt, blouse, and Indian vest. "We'll leave this darling hat right here so it won't get crushed." And she led Evelyn out, who looked more miserable than ever. I gave her a wink, and she smiled bravely.

"Well, Nathan, I'd say we're almost out of here. Just a quick turn around the room, a canapé or two, a gentle good-bye to Mom, and we can—"

Suddenly, a squeal at the door caused Morgan to lose his footing and stumble onto the bed.

"Morgan?! MORGAN! Hi! It's me! *Cookie*! Cookie *McPherson*! Remember? The Rockette? I was in your summer class last year? I did Portia?"

"Oh, of course! Cookie!"

I gazed appreciatively at Cookie, who was—as numerous writers might say—"a tall drink of water." Her short tight dress impressed the fact rather consistently. Her long golden hair reached to her waist. Her breasts were uplifted in a gentle and inviting curve.

("Really, Nathan—*inviting?*" Morgan asked later, reading over my early drafts at my urging. I nodded solemnly.)

"You're not going to believe this. I ACTUALLY AM GOING TO PLAY *PORTIA!*"

"You are? Terrific!"

"In a scene. I'll be on a stage, and there will be an audience. I'm really excited. Arnold—the artistic director—said I was wonderful! I just did everything you said. I get to cut my thigh, but not really. You know what we're going to do? We're going to get a knife but first really dull the edge then put like lipstick really thick on it, and then the *knife* is in actuality going to just put the *lipstick* on my thigh! Isn't that incredible? The director is here somewhere. You should meet him."

"No, that's all right. I can't stay long. I just wanted to bring Ev—my mother. She has trouble with . . . with night vision."

"Oh!" Cookie's own eyes grew round and luminous. She sank on the bed. Morgan stood hurriedly.

"Yes, it is quite unfortunate really. Something to do with carrots. That is, not enough of them. Which can be corrected easily, it seems, if she would just, you know, eat more carrots."

I could see beads of sweat on his forehead. I tried to be helpful. "Morgan, take off your jacket," I whispered.

"No. No, we're not staying, Nathan."

"Nathan?"

"Oh, I'm sorry. Nathan, let me introduce Cookie, a very—a unique actress. Cookie, this is Nathan."

"God, you are really adorable!"

Now it was my turn to feel nervous. I jumped off the bed.

"Cookie, where are you?" a woman's voice called from the corridor. When she appeared, she revealed herself to be a second tall drink of water. "MORGAN?" she squealed, standing momentarily as frozen as the two daiquiris she held carefully in front of her. Startled, Morgan fell on the bed again, this time on Evelyn's hat.

"*Yes!*" screamed Cookie. "Morgan, remember Mandy? Mandy gave me your name originally, in the beginning, because she studied with you the summer *before*."

"Of course! Mandy! Mandy, how are you?"

"YOU'RE NOT GOING TO BELIEVE THIS! Here's your drink, honey." She handed a daiquiri to Cookie. "This is so majorly awesome because Cheryl and I—" She stepped back into the hallway. "CHERYL, COME HERE! YOU'LL NEVER GUESS!" And stepping back into the room, she continued, "Morgan, we were just *talking* about you!"

Whereupon Cheryl, yet *another* talk drink of water, entered to peer over Mandy's well-formed and spaghetti-strapped shoulder.

"Cheryl, this is Morgan, who I was talking about like five minutes ago. Remember I was telling you about this majorly incredible teacher I went to one summer at the Academy? This is him!"

"*NO!*" Cheryl screamed, sipping her champagne. "*THAT'S AMAZING!*"

"Morgan, this is Cheryl. I swear to God, not more than five minutes ago we were talking about you. Cheryl is going to start acting. She's been managing a health club, but I went there and told her that you're a genius, honestly, and she's going to call you because I remember you said sometimes you coach like when I had that audition for Samsonite."

"Oh, that is really a fairly rare—"

Mandy sat down next to Morgan, just missing Evelyn's hat which Morgan had removed from beneath him and which frankly did not look any the worse for having been sat upon.

"I mean it, Morgan. That hour I spent with you, it was like I was actually learning to act. I mean for the first time," Mandy said solemnly. "Wasn't it like that, Cookie? Didn't I say that to you, and you said it was the same for you?"

"I did," Cookie said solemnly. "Of course, for me, it actually *was* the first time."

"God, I would *love* to act for the first time with Morgan," Cheryl said softly, sitting down at his feet. "First times are so special."

Morgan began to hyperventilate.

"Anyway, Cheryl, you've *got* to work with Morgan. We did this thing. I don't know what you call it exactly, but the idea was that you were actually talking to someone. What do you call that exercise, Morgan?" Mandy made a charming moue as she concentrated.

"Oh, I guess, you know, basically I call that talking to someone."

"YOU SEE WHAT I MEAN?" Mandy shrieked. "A GENIUS! I really think I got the commercial because I acted like I was talking to someone about Samsonite. No. Wait!" She shot her well-toned arms out, poising them dramatically and gracefully in space. We waited. "I didn't *act* like I was talking to someone. I *was* talking to someone. Oh my god! I think I get it!"

"Talking to someone. God," Cheryl said.

Mandy turned to me. "Hello."

"Hello," I answered.

"A Rockette's professional life is kind of short. I mean we shouldn't really get old, if we can help it."

"Or hurt." Cookie nodded.

"So we have to basically figure out how to transition," added Cheryl. She sighed. "I'm managing a health club right now, but it's just not the same as the Radio City Christmas Spectacular."

"OF COURSE NOT, HONEY!" said Mandy. That's why you must work with Morgan."

"Could I take a class, do you think?" asked Mandy shyly.

"Of course you could," said Morgan who had gotten his breathing under control and now felt the easiest way to escape would be to act as if this welter of profound femininity was a normal occurrence. "Unfortunately, classes won't start up again until January."

"WHAT ABOUT PRIVATELY?" Mandy and Cookie said in unison.

"Oh. Well. Yes. On occasion—"

"Privately!" said Cheryl in a soft voice, but a thrilling one nonetheless. "What should I wear?"

"Nathan, where are you going?" Morgan called desperately as I headed for the door.

"Off for some champagne, Morgan. I'll be fine."

Morgan started to follow, but suddenly, there was another squeal at the door.

"MORGAN? MORGAN, I CAN'T BELIEVE—" All the women screamed together, introducing the fourth who needed no introduction because she too had taken a class with Morgan.

I trotted happily down the hallway and headed back into the softly lit living room where a large low coffee table held numerous slices of bread and cheeses. I settled into a beige leather couch which resembled a large mass of baking-powder biscuit dough and briefly disappeared until it exhaled, allowing me to resurface.

"You darling thing! Here!" A lovely Teutonic beauty handed me a glass of champagne, and I sipped it gratefully. I sampled brie on a digestive biscuit and contentedly looked at all the happy people gesticulating, making majorly deep points with each other and so on while a modern jazz beat thumped in the background, helping me to hearken—however dimly—back to my own African roots.

"Hello. For those of you who don't know me, my name is Arnold Freitag."

I turned to see a young man seated to my left in the deep recesses of the leather couch. He held a bottle of Michelob and stared into space, speaking to no one.

"Hello," I said politely.

"Hello. My name is Arnold Freitag. Here is my card. I am the artistic director of DUMP. We are a small nonprofit theater company dedicated to artistic growth in and around the community by stretching our artistic muscles and developing new works which speak through and into the soul of the collective humanity, where the new voice of the artist can find itself and seek fulfillment while making the world better and putting an end to grief and intolerance. We do this through a main stage series of old and new works, a workshop series for the future main stage series, and a reading series for the future workshop series as well as an Arts in Education Program and our international wing where we hope to set up a theater in Djibouti. Or Kiev."

"Sounds like an extraordinary company."

"Oh, it is. Especially when you consider we only have five core members."

"Five!" I exclaimed. "You must all keep rather busy."

"Yes, so far it's just me, a gal I met at Berkley, her girlfriend, my roommate who majored in philosophy, and a friend who runs a travel agency who always wanted to do theater. But we're growing. Each show we do, two or three people want to stay on."

"Are you doing anything now? That we might be able to come and see?"

"Are you in the theater?"

"Well, my mentor is."

"A *mentor*. Cool. We are, in point of fact, developing a mentor program. But so far, it's only in the planning stages because we would have to add to the company so there would be something for someone to head up. May I ask who your mentor is?"

"Morgan Johansson."

"Morgan. *The* Morgan Johansson?

I suddenly remembered how Morgan always made reservations under another name, and while I assumed it was a romantic thing to do (in a sweet espionage sort of way), I never realized that it actually made his life easier. I experienced an even deeper respect for my mentor and, I will admit, deep respect in being associated with him. However, the moment of deep respect was followed immediately by the realization that I was now probably in deep trouble.

"Whose last year's *Out, Out, Brief Candle* totally rocked the off-off-Broadway scene and *Ducks Have Mothers Too* was the beginning of Supalady's incredible career. Do you know he got a gig on *Friends* after that?

"Uh . . ."

"Is he here?"

"Well, actually—"

"Gosh, it would mean a lot to everyone if Mr. Johansson could come and maybe be on our board of directors—or if he's too busy, on our letterhead."

"Well, perhaps you could give me a flyer and I'll see what I can do."

"Sure. We're doing a series of scenes from Shakespeare. We're calling it *From Bard to Verse.*"

"That's very good." I smiled, suddenly hopeful that perhaps this man was not the roaring nut that he appeared. And I was hoping, as well, that Morgan would stay rooted in the midst of his harem long enough for me to lose Arnold, thereby keeping Morgan anonymous and myself not glowered at.

"Hiya, pal." Morgan eased himself into the leather couch and was lost to us for a brief moment and then reappeared. "I completely forgot that one summer when the Academy had so many Rockettes unaccountably enrolled. You know, I've only ever had champagne once and I lost the use of my knees for several hours, but I think I could use a glass."

"Are you Morgan Johansson, who last year directed a definitive version of the Scottish Play using the witches as a girl band?"

"Uh . . ." Morgan looked at me.

"Have my champagne. I've barely touched it," I said quickly.

"My name is Arnold Freitag, and I am the artistic director of DUMP, a nonprofit theater company dedicated to the development—"

"Here is a flyer," I said hurriedly, knowing that if Morgan heard what I had heard, he might toss the gentle yet certifiably insane young man out the window. "*From Bard to Verse!* Isn't that clever, Morgan?"

The Teutonic beauty handed me another glass of champagne. I smiled. Morgan glowered.

"Arnold, what does DUMP stand for?" I asked nervously.

"Don't Under Mine Peace."

"I see," I said. "How . . . earnest."

"MORGAN!" Madeleine had arrived. "Darling, we haven't had a moment to chat all evening! Did you know that your mother and I lived together when we first came to New York? Then her career started and I married . . . someone . . . a doctor, I think." She insinuated her lithe body against Morgan's. I was very grateful to Madeleine, for in pressuring her lovely thighs against Morgan, she took a great deal of pressure off me.

"Of course, you know all that. But did you know also that I am very, very drunk?" Madeleine was tossing her head as if to toss her hair out of her eyes, even as the cloud of cotton candy stayed imperturbably in place.

"Uh-huh," whispered Morgan, taking a rather large gulp of champagne.

"And it's my birthday."

"Yes, happy—"

"Did you bring me a present?"

"Yes. Actually, we brought—"

"I know your *mother* brought me a present, but I was wondering if you brought me something extra, extra, extra special?"

("Nathan," Morgan said sternly to me the next day while reading this chapter. "I don't know why you think your readers need to know about this."

"Morgan," I countered crisply, "I am writing a chronicle of our time, and I mustn't start censoring myself."

"I see," Morgan harrumphed.)

("Nathan," Morgan said sternly to me three days later when he read the rewrites of this chapter, "I have never, in my life, harrumphed.

"Morgan," I said sternly and yet with affection, "*cool your jets.*")

Suddenly there was a lot of "shushing" and a resultant decrescendo of party noises coming from another area of this palatial apartment. The four of us turned to look but saw only backs of other party-goers. Morgan tried to use the moment to escape but the champagne had indeed gone to his knees and he hadn't the strength to jettison himself from the couch. Instead he sank deeper, taking more of Madeleine with him.

"Ooooooooh!" she said happily.

"SHUSH!" several guests reprimanded.

Suddenly we heard the opening introduction to "I'd Rather Be Blue Over You" on piano. All delinquent party noises were snuffed immediately to hear a gutsy, smoky, alto voice. Before the song resolved itself, however, the singer segued into "Smoke Gets in Your Eyes" followed by "What's New?" and ending with "When I Fall in Love." Much enthusiastic clapping ensued, and I trumpeted madly. Even Arnold emerged from his rhetoric to stand and clap and allowed me to stand on his shoulder so I could see.

"Gorgeous. Absolutely gorgeous," said Morgan. "Who was that?"

"Oh, you big funny!" Madeleine cooed in Morgan's ear, for he was still unable to wrest himself from the couch. "That was your mom."

"My mom?" Morgan asked, the champagne clearly having gone to his head.

"Yes! That sweet lady you came with tonight!" Madeleine burbled merrily at her wit.

"Oh yes! Of course." Morgan shook his head as if to clear it.

"You big funny!" Whereupon Madeleine stuck her tongue in Morgan's ear.

"Aaaaaaggggggghhhhhhhhffffffff!" screamed Morgan, toppling to his left and rolling off the couch onto the floor, very much in the manner first-aid books instruct us to behave if we have caught fire.

"Nathan, we should go!" He tried to stagger to his feet.

"Okay," I said, peering down at him from Arnold's shoulder.

"Let me help you, Mr. Johansson." Arnold lifted him rather effortlessly.

"I'm fine," Morgan said. "I just need to get my jacket."

"And our startling array of goods from Bed, Bath, and Beyond," I reminded him.

"Okay," Arnold said, steering him toward the bedroom. But then we were caught in a small eddy of people and thus propelled toward the piano where Evelyn was sitting and chatting volubly with those around her.

"Mrs. Wambaugh! May I just say what an honor it was to have you grace our evening with such a deeply felt yet whimsical medley?" said Arnold gravely.

"Thank you. Thank you very much."

"And what an honor it is as well to meet you at last. My name is Arnold Freitag, and I'm artistic director of DUMP, a small nonprofit theater company dedicated to—"

I gently kicked Arnold in the head. He stopped.

"Here is my card," he offered. "In case you would ever like a venue on the fringe, so to speak."

"A venue on the fringe," Evelyn repeated, looking at the card. "That would be an excellent name for your experimental wing."

"Gosh! We forgot all about having an experimental wing!" Arnold said, hitting his forehead in that characteristic gesture that needs no description here.

"I see you've met my son."

"YOUR SON! HOLY COW! THIS IS ABSOLUTELY INCREDIBLE!"
I kicked Arnold softly in the head again, and he returned to
lowercase. "Two majorly famous people whom I frankly idolize turn
out to be related!"

"Hiya, Arnold!" Cookie had made her way to the piano. "Oh, you've
met Morgan. Morgan, this is the director of the show I'm in. Who
thought I was so fantastic. Morgan was my acting teacher," she said
proudly to Arnold.

"HOLY COW! I DON'T BELIEVE IT! THIS IS KISMET!" Arnold shouted.

Cookie looked around briefly, thinking Arnold was introducing his
date. Not seeing her, she shrugged and turned to Evelyn. "Could
you do 'Send in the Clowns'?"

"Sure, honey." Evelyn said.

While Evelyn began the intro and Cookie sat on the piano with her
perfect legs crossed, Morgan grabbed me off Arnold's shoulder and
we disappeared into the crowd. "We're outta here, pal," Morgan said.

We pushed our way back into the bedroom, first peering in carefully
to make sure no one—at least no one of the female persuasion—was
already there, and then tiptoed in. Morgan sat on the edge of the
bed with his head in his hands. "My god," he said. "My god."

I let him breathe deeply for a moment, thinking—all things
considered—I should be quiet.

"Okay, let me find my jacket and we're off."

Morgan proceeded to dig deeply into the coats, but the jacket
seemed to be missing. I searched through the pile as well, but
Morgan's beautiful brown suede jacket was gone.

"How do you like that, pal? We come into what may be the most chic neighborhood in the city and someone walks off with my jacket. See anything you like?"

I had my eye on a beautiful black velvet swing coat that I thought would look wonderful on Doris when, suddenly, the door opened and a stunningly lovely young woman was standing in the room with us. Her hair had been piled on her head in a French twist but by now had come down slightly so that tendrils framed her face, pale against her dark hair. Her large eyes were highlighted in beautiful blue liner, her mouth painted in a rich shiny coral hue. She wore a simple black dress short enough to reveal a pair of lovely legs highlighted by sparkling black heels.

At this point my mind registered three surprises at the same time. The first was that she chose to accessorize such glamour with a purse made out of license plates. The second was that she had on Morgan's suede jacket. And the third was that she was Abby.

"Oh, hello, Morgan and Nathan. I seem to have taken the wrong coat."

"Ah," said Morgan.

She took it off, placed it gently on the bed, and picked up the velvet swing coat.

"Easy to get those two confused," Morgan said, helping her into her coat.

"Oh well. Sometimes my mind gets on other things, you see," she said, embarrassed. "I was halfway home in the cab when I noticed. Thank you for not being upset. You are very kind."

She turned and looked at Morgan. He at her. I held my breath. I remembered the quote on the napkin. Maybe this was going to be the "after that" that was supposed to happen at the Cloisters when love happened in a moment and what happened after that hadn't.

"Abby! Abby, here you are!"

In a stunning moment of history repeating itself, Jeremy came into the room.

"Oh! Jeremy! Hi!"

"*Hi?* Where have you been all evening?"

"Oh . . . around. Here and there. You know. It was a crowded party."

"I thought you must have left!"

"Left?! How silly!" Abby looked at Morgan quickly, then at me, then at Jeremy.

"I just know how much you loathe parties and that you were perfectly capable of diving into a cab."

"Oh really! What an eccentric notion!" Abby managed a brief laugh. Wanting to be helpful, I emitted a small burble. Jeremy scowled absently.

"Then why do you have on your coat?" Jeremy asked, digging through the pile for his.

Suddenly, Arnold entered with a tray of cake and coffee. "Here, Mr. Johansson. Feeling better?"

"Thank you, yes, and please stop calling me Mr. Johansson."

"Here, Nathan."

"Thank you, Arnold."

"Here, Abby, have some cake."

"Thank you, Arnold," Abby said, taking a slice and settling onto a settee.

I was about to ask Arnold how he knew Abby but then, remembering how my natural curiosity had gotten me into a bit of trouble this evening, decided silence was the better part of valor.

"Darling, we must be off! We're meeting the Rosenbaums at Un Deux Trois."

Once again, I had occasion to muse on Jeremy's fascination with numbers.

"Coffee, Mr. Johansson."

"Yes, thank you, Arnold." Morgan sat down on the bed.

Evelyn entered, looking exhausted, and sat on the bed just missing her hat.

"Here, Mrs. Wambaugh, take my cake and coffee. I haven't touched them," Arnold said.

"Oh no, Arnold, I couldn't."

"Mrs. Wambaugh, I cannot tell you what an honor it would be if, at some point in my future, I could turn to someone—my young son perhaps—and say that one night I gave Evelyn Wambaugh my untouched coffee and cake."

We all paused, forks and cups in midair, feet in midstep, arms in midsleeves, all touched by verbiage which would have seemed inflated on paper. And yet with Arnold's honest intention, every word rang with a rare and simple truth.

"Arnold, thank you," Evelyn said simply, and indeed dove into her cake with sudden appetite.

"Well then, will you guys be going to see *From Bard to Verse*, do you suppose?" Abby asked Morgan casually as she finished her cake and put on a pair of crushed red velvet gloves.

Morgan gazed into her eyes, suddenly hypnotized. "Yes, we will."

"Holy cow!" Arnold said, but I cautioned him with a glance to stay quiet, for I sensed that his enthusiasm could trample any and all opportunities that the universe was beginning to extend his way.

"Let's hurry, darling!" Jeremy fitted his fingers into a pair of tight Italian leather gloves. I wondered if, in a minute, he was going to pull out a pair of sunglasses and tell us his Maserati was doubled parked.

"I'm a little worried about the Alfa Romeo. Even in this neighborhood."

Abby centered her gaze on Morgan, the moment suddenly suspended for two and that one who, by mere luck, has become a chronicler of our time.

"*Now*, darling," said Jeremy. And in a very proprietorial fashion, he escorted Abby out of the room.

All continued as before, although perhaps for one of us, not *quite* as before.

For while Evelyn and Arnold chatted shyly about the possibilities of a venue on the fringe and I continued to be grateful for the superb Ghirardelli chocolate shavings on my piece of hazelnut cake, Morgan gazed absently and bemusedly at the bedroom door—a door which, perhaps, had at last opened on his own musty attic, pouring in a sweet, long-absent light.

Theoria

My solo journey today had a twofold purpose: to find a perfect gift for Morgan's birthday and to treat myself to Café des Artistes—a dark, well-appointed, and eclectic eating establishment which had become a favorite of mine, wherein one might encounter a group of artistes, their berets set at rakish angles, speaking volubly about Cubism, pathetic fallacy, myth, and politics in a haze of unfiltered and aromatic cigarettes. The Café would *also* serve two purposes: a small but tasty collation and the place wherein I would begin my novel.

For though I agree with Morgan that the previous pages have technically been *written*, I did *not* believe that the mere description of my new adventures—hapless and anecdotal though they are, and admittedly told from my unique perspective—would ever be enough for the one who, though still an abstraction, has all of my affection. That one, of course, being the reader.

Also, I had seen on Morgan's shelf, right next to *A Child's Garden of Verses*, a book entitled *Writing in Restaurants*. I felt the actual *reading* of the book was not necessary for the advice given so freely on its cover already had spoken to me, and I felt a restaurant was exactly what my imagination required.

Even though it was only mid-October, I felt a sudden nip in the air that presaged the coming of Old Man Winter, and so thought suddenly to purchase for myself the above-mentioned item of haberdashery. I stopped at Julio's folding table on the corner.

Julio beamed his hello and happily offered a lovely purple beret for the low, low price of seven dollars. The purchase made quickly and my beret now perched on my pate, I continued to browse, having discovered journeying with Morgan that life can rise up and greet us in unaccountable ways—and indeed can change lives, as this very chronicle has indicated and will continue to do so (hopefully with a minimum of redundancy) if we simply go slowly and consider the notion of *Theoria*.

"Did you say Peoria?" asked a sweet older woman attired in the senior citizen's ubiquitous nylon jogging suit and Nikes. She was carrying two large shopping bags, looking harried and tired the way people do when they have gotten off a chartered bus from Connecticut.

"No, no, I said *theoria*," I answered, still looking about. If there was a gift for Morgan on Julio's table, I wanted to procure it and be on my way, for I was anxious to begin my novel and was looking forward to salami on a crisp baguette.

"Oh! One of my daughters lives in Peoria." She was looking carefully at a large plastic head of Elvis with a light bulb in the center. "What do you think of this?" she asked me. "*Honestly.*"

"Well," I considered. "I think it manages a boldness in its aesthetic as well as an insouciance in its function. A happy addition to any family room."

"I liked it immediately," she confided.

"Then you must have it." I returned to browsing.

"Yes. Everyone else is having lunch at the Edison Hotel before *Crazy for You*, but I thought, 'Darn it. I go to New York to go to *New York*, not to be insulated by my own kind!'"

"Why, you've come at least thirty blocks south already!" I said.

"Oh well, yes, I just get lost with walking and with acquiring, I suppose."

"And thus you are rewarded for your own boldness, your own insouciance."

"What a lovely way with words you have. Are you a writer by any chance?" she asked shyly, getting out her wallet and paying Julio.

"Oh no, I . . ." And here I struggled, for I could hear Morgan's gentle reminder of my state of grace, yet I could also hear dear Sidney Cox saying "one is not a writer until one has sold something." I thought for a moment then bridged the two. "I am one in the making."

"Oh, good for you! Good for *you*! My name is Sadie."

"Very pleased to meet you, Sadie. My name is Nathan."

"And where exactly is *theoria* then? If you don't mind my asking, if it isn't too personal, if, as a New Yorker, you need to keep yourself protected more vigorously than such a conversation would allow." Sadie peered at me through her large trifocals, encased in pink pastel frames, her arm cradling Elvis's larger-than-life-size head.

"Oh well, it isn't actually so much a place as a state." I then realized what with New York and Connecticut being in the air, this explanation was not helpful. "That is, the state of having vision, of being able to see."

"Ah," she said. "Yes." And suddenly catching sight of the Empire State Building, she was suddenly stilled. I understood, for even I who see it at least once a day feel the need to point it out to Morgan whenever I glimpse its elegant majesty, as if I have suddenly caught sight of a celebrity. Feeling that our conversation had managed the farthest bounds of its conditional intimacy, I sidled off to peruse Julio's startling array of items, which today included watches, socks, appointment books, comic books, a dartboard, and a Black and Decker iron. I had about given up the notion of the perfect gift when suddenly, from beneath the table, I espied a set of plastic bowling pins, still in their original packaging, that would go nicely in our lengthy hallway. I had, for a while, suspected that both Morgan and I could do with a bit more exercise, and as the notion of joining a health club was even more unacceptable to Morgan than owning a car, this seemed a perfect and whimsical solution. I turned to say good-bye to Sadie who still stood gazing at the Empire State Building. Perhaps, in retrospect, her next sentence was not really the non sequitur it seemed at the time.

"I have twelve children."

I paused in midstep. "Twelve? As in . . . *twelve?*"

"Doce?" asked Julio, beginning to package up the iron for another customer, now suddenly startled into stillness.

"Doce niños?" asked the buyer of the iron who had been gently bouncing a stroller up and down to keep her own niño content.

"DAAAACCCAAAAA!" confirmed the baby.

"Si, doce," said Sadie, her eyes still fastened on man's all too thinly disguised symbol of his potent energies.

All of us strangers, all of us knitted for a brief moment by such an unexpected disclosure we could do nothing but answer with a slim, awe-filled silence. Then I cleared my throat.

"Well," I said, "you look *great.*"

"Oh, thank you. Four were twins. So, technically, that is only eight pregnancies. And after about seven or eight children, it doesn't really matter. I mean they are *people*, after all, so they begin to help out, if for no other reason than their own survival. And really, you have to start being a bit more casual about things. You know— measles, colic, formulas, latent reading skills, tantrums, rebellious behavior. I mean you have to, or you will just *explode*."

"Well, how lovely for you then to have this day out for yourself."

"Oh, they are mostly all out of the house now. Just my youngest son who is now twenty and is just *lost*. And frankly—oh, and I hate to admit this, but his problems just bore me now."

"Of course. You've been through eleven sets of problems. It must have gotten repetitive."

"Oh, it did. It did. You try and remind yourself that this person is saying it for the first time for himself, but you've heard it a hundred times already, so you put on an interested face, but really, you just want to get your nails done or get a new slip cover for the couch. But he's at a community college, so he's out of the house a lot. And four months ago, my husband left me for a younger woman . . . so." She shrugged, as if perhaps this gentle gesture could jettison her grief.

What with my new beret which had suddenly begun to feel a bit constrictive, my growing need of a small collation, the awkwardness of now having to carry a bowling set larger than myself, and my sudden rage at a sweet woman's dismissal, I shouted perhaps a trifle insensitively, "WELL, I CERTAINLY HOPE *SHE'S* READY TO DELIVER THE GOODS!"

Sadie's gaze at last now wrested from afar, she turned to face me. Her befuddled countenance suddenly broke into a large smile, followed by hearty laughter. Then Julio began to laugh and turned to the woman who bought the iron. "Dijo que espera que este lista para cumplir con lo prometido!"

"Si, si! the woman agreed, covering her mouth with her hand and laughing in a knowing way.

"DAACCAAAADAAAAA!" burbled the baby.

I didn't particularly feel like laughing, but I was happy that the others did, especially the lady with the lamp, she with her own *theoria* and the courage to step out from her covey of similarly attired senior citizens, to peruse the wonders of New York, to make contact with (as I now saw myself) a somewhat self-involved elephant in a beret who could *talk* more easily about *theoria* than *experience* it. Whatever kind of writer was I going to be if I couldn't recognize the actual miracles that the streets presented? I sat down on my bag of pins to matter this out.

"The reason I asked if you were a writer is, well, I've written a play," Sadie said shyly.

"My goodness. Well, you certainly have a unique perspective. On just about anything," I added.

"And I wondered if you could give me any hints on how to have it produced."

"Well." And now I admit, perhaps I was a trifle overanxious to make up for any brusqueness in my earlier conversation. "As a matter of fact, I live with a gentleman who has been a mentor to several contemporary playwrights." (If she wondered how he could mentor any other kind of playwright, she was too polite to mention it.)

"No! Really? A *mentor*!"

"And he has been asked to be on the board of a very up-and-coming theater company."

"Oh my goodness! Up-and-coming! How could I get in touch with him, do you think?"

"Here is his card." I proffered it adroitly.

"Oh my god! He has a *card*! Oh, you don't know what this means! You don't know what this means! Oh, it is my lucky day! It truly is! Oh! Oh, but the time! I must get up to the theater! Oh, I do so thank you for everything." She hailed a cab, loaded her acquisitions into the backseat. I watched the two heads in the backseat—one well-coifed, the other plastic—looking for all the world as if they were having an intriguing conversation.

I sighed, hoisted my pins, waved good-bye to Julio, and headed to the café, feeling that I had somehow managed to redeem my initial self-involvement. After all, my self-involvement had actually centered around finding Morgan's birthday present; so in a way, it was a kind of *selfless* involvement. And even if that sweet woman *did* see her way to sending her manuscript (an activity I truly doubted would come to pass, as my memory of life in Connecticut contained such things as lawn maintenance, car maintenance, home maintenance, bridge parties, and volunteering at the local hospital), it would take Morgan all of one hour some evening to look over the play and sketch down a few comments. And it might even be good.

Indeed, by the time I had entered the café, I had Morgan directing the most acclaimed new play of the season, both of us genially present at the Tony Awards, silk scarves in place. I waved to Marissa who was serving a few people outside beneath the café's brightly striped awning, die-hard patrons who refused to allow the change in season to inhibit their joy of outdoor dining, and headed into the rich familiar darkness of the café's back room—a room in which Michelangelo, Monet, Strindberg, and Ring Lardner would all be comfortable imbibing while filling with raucous and passionate debates.

As the sunlight had been quite thorough, I stumbled against numerous heavy wooden tables until I gratefully fell into my favorite chair that I hoped might have once cradled the derrière of an Italian bishop. As my eyes became more accustomed, I detected the dark oil paintings of voluptuous women, fruits, lutes, and gourds on the walls.

"Mon elephant, bonjour. Ça va?" asked Marissa, a willowy beauty.

"Oui ça va bien aujourd'hui. Et vous?"

"Très bien aussi." She smiled warmly. I ordered a glass of Pinot Grigio and a salami on a baguette. As she smiled and left, I felt again how astonishing it was that New York City was filled with so many women. All of them in different sizes, shapes, and colors, with different languages and accents, accessories and ideas, yet all of them so extraordinarily beautiful—be it Marissa with her lips outlined in deep magenta as they were today, Sadie with her trifocals, Abby with her raven hair piled atop her head, Evelyn with her smoky rich contralto, or my dear Doris, whose charms simply were too infinite and deeply felt by me to be parceled into this list.

I paused and scratched my head and felt a bit fitful that my surroundings were always infinitely more intriguing than any thoughts in my head.

I heaved a sigh and began the daunting task of beginning. I decided on a working title.

Mon Elephant, Bonjour

I liked it. So far, things were going well. Now for a first sentence that would induce the reader to keep reading.

The sky was low and glowering, and Marlene—pregnant with her seventh child—bit her lip in consternation. Why had she answered the request to visit the old forsaken estate which was so monstrously, so bleakly dilapidated, with the possible exception of the beautifully manicured lawn, on this night of all possible nights? A wolf howled; trees trembled in the preface of a coming storm.

Indeed, her antique earrings with amethyst stones surrounded by tiny pearls shook in sudden empathy with all of nature.

or

Dave Edwards, sleek and dapper, eyed himself in the mirror of the men's room at Pete's Place while he heard a husky contralto belt out "Cry Me a River" in the bar beyond, and liked what he saw. The facial reconstruction was good. Not only did he bear no resemblance to his former self, but he was now suddenly, for the first time in his life, immensely attractive. What would life be like if all women looked at him the way that beauty with raven hair and teal-framed glasses did just now?

or

Polly Fairbanks, crippled since a mysterious bowling accident seven years ago, wheeled herself onto the patio to peer through her binoculars at the black-capped heron which had mysteriously begun to nest in her father's Japanese garden some four days ago. Imagine her astonishment as she gazed out in the yard and saw, wedged tightly in the vortex of an old apple tree—

"Pinot Grigio et salami, oui?"

"Oui, merci," I said, grateful for the interruption. For my beret had started to itch, and I wasn't sure what exactly to wedge in the vortex of the tree. I was happy with my work so far, as all three sentences seemed good openers. I sunk my teeth happily into the hard crusty roll and looked about.

Perhaps it was owing to the initial darkness that my eyes had not fastened earlier on a woman slumped over a table in what seemed to be a state of unconsciousness in a far corner beneath the painting of a huge black-capped heron.

I bit my lip in consternation, for had I yet *again* become so self-involved that I was blind to the real drama and genuine distress of the world around me? If this was the case, if I could not begin to balance the two, then the life of a writer was going to be too big a price to pay.

I trotted over to her and leaped up onto the table. "Are you all right?" I asked.

"Hmmmmm?"

"Are you all right?"

"Yeah. Fine. Probably. Maybe not." She slurred her words and attempted to rouse herself, shaking her head as if to clear it, just as I had seen Morgan do the night of Madeleine's party, a gesture that seemed to me both instinctual and useless.

Her hair was oddly sharply cropped. One eyebrow was pierced. She had heavy green eye shadow, her eyes overly outlined in heavy black which only served to emphasize the deep circles under her eyes. She wore a bright but shabby scarf, and her hands were encased in odd lace gloves, the fingertips cut out. Though there was an original (if rather gruesome) élan to her ensemble, the overall impression was that the woman was in the midst of a dreadful hangover.

"How long have I been here?" she asked suddenly.

"I don't know."

"How long have *you* been here?"

"About twenty minutes."

"Did you see me come in?"

"No."

"So I've been here more than twenty minutes."

"Yes!" I said with a certainty I did not feel, for hadn't I proven to myself twice already today that looking *outward* was not my strong suit?

"Where are we?"

"We are at Café Des Artistes, in the Village in New York City." This, at least, I could say with complete conviction.

"That's right. I remember."

"How many of these have you had?" I asked gently, gesturing toward the wineglass and hoping there was no judgment in my voice.

"One."

"One!" I said, shocked. "Well, you certainly have a delicate system."

I could see her eyes brightening. They were a special shade of brown. The color of root beer. Where had I seen—

"Jesus Christ! He put something in my drink!"

This was unexpected. She looked into her glass that clearly had held red wine, perhaps a cabernet, but indeed there were dregs that were not of a cork's making. Marissa was a professional sommelier and would not allow her wines to be tainted by sloppy decantation.

The woman put her head in her hands. "I knew New York was going to be a problem for me. I begged for anything else. I would have taken *Albania* even."

"Uh-huh," I said in what I hoped was a comforting fashion. This was indeed inspiring to me, for Sidney Cox had said if one lives in a heightened way, one need not be heightened to write. I was feeling my living was being heightened by the minute, and the return to my novel was going to be easier than its inception. As the woman sat up, she gazed deeply at nothing, which meant she was gazing inward, willing her mental wheels to grind into gear.

Now the woman looked at me closely for the first time.

"You're an elephant."

"That's right. Nathan."

"Nathan what?"

"Nathan Emmanuel." I hesitated. "Christ."

"CHRIST?!"

Marissa looked in. "Everything is all right here?"

"Oui! Deux tasses du cafés. Noir, si vous plait." I added, surprised at the clear directive of my voice and rather proud of the accent as well.

"Well, I'll be damned." And the youngish woman smiled, her brown eyes now as luminous as Cookie's. Suddenly, I felt that her odd hair, the piercing, the makeup, the entire outfit was not really her at all. Perhaps it was a disguise. *Could* it be a disguise? But why?

"What is your name?" I asked pleasantly.

"My name?" the woman asked.

"Yes. Your name," I repeated. Perhaps I was right the first time and the woman's brain had been destroyed by a life on the street.

Marissa brought the coffees.

"Merci," the young woman said. "Serait-ce possible pour moi utiliser votre téléphone? Je suis désolé pour vous déranger de quelque façon mais c'est très important. Je dois vous demander de me fier sur ceci."

Marissa eyed this young woman who perhaps had no business being in an establishment of such class, and yet she recognized something genuine. It could be that the woman's perfect French was enough to win her over, for the French especially love those who take the time to completely absorb their language and culture. And who could blame them? If there is one language and culture I would—

"Absolument. Le téléphone est en bas le hall près des salles de bains."

"Merci." She got up to go.

"Uh, I wonder if you could tell me your name?" I asked again.

"Do you have a card by any chance?" she asked me.

"Why, as a matter of fact—"

"May I have two of them?"

"Well, of course, but—"

"I'll be right back."

"But—"

"Do they have dessert here?"

"Yes, as a matter of—"

"Do they have tiramisu?"

"Yes, they do. I know because it is—"

"Great. It's my favorite. Order me a piece."

"All right, but—"

And taking Morgan's last two business cards from me, she was gone. I was frankly delighted that she shared my passion for tiramisu, and feeling a bit exhilarated by all that had gone on, I trotted back to my opening three sentences, invigorated by the past, excited about the future that dessert would bring.

> Marlene lifted the large and heavy brass knocker and let it resound against the large and heavy oaken door. She could hear what sounded like the dreadful scuffling of sea claws along an ocean floor. Finally, the door opened to reveal a small wizened gentleman, clothed in traditional Jesuit garb except for the large clip-on aerator sandals strapped to his feet. Marlene suddenly became aware of a pregnant pause, noted the irony, stilled the terror in her heart, and willed herself to the adroit conversational gambits made famous by her family.
>
> "Well!" she said, a sunny smile belying her inner terror. "Now I see why your lawn is so lovely!"

*　　*　　*

But his ruminations on the raven-haired beauty with teal-framed glasses went no further, for a shot rang out, shattering the mirror to smithereens. It was instantaneous, but not so instantaneous that Dave had not had a chance to catch the reflection of the shooter in the mirror, giving him a chance to duck for protection behind a stall door. Pulling out his own gun, saying a brief thank-you to St. Jude, he reflected—not without noting the irony—that he was a lost cause to end lost causes.

*　　*　　*

. . . . a saucepan, glinting in the late afternoon sun.

I felt all three openings had possibility for *Mon Elephant, Bonjour*. And after I picked one, I obviously had the beginnings of the next two books in the series. Feeling very proud of myself, I took a sip of coffee and suddenly realized that the woman had been gone too long, our tiramisu had never arrived, and the front room which had happily punctuated our time here with the characteristic hiss of a cappuccino machine and clinking of glasses and chopping of lettuce was now oddly, eerily silent. With a sudden fear, I hurried in to find the front room in complete confusion, Marissa unconscious, and my new groggy friend being forced into a Lincoln Town Car by two burly and vacant beasts. I cursed my state of grace, for it had made me once again oblivious to life around me, although that oblivion might have been due in no small part to having stuffed my ears into this confounded beret.

I raced out into the street. "Unhand her, you villains!" I shouted. Gunshots rang out, hitting the spindly legs that supported the awning. It tumbled down, people screamed, fruit rolled, dogs barked, and all was in darkness.

Mayhem Somewhat Resolved

"Nathan! Are you all right?" Morgan made his way through several policemen toward me and Marissa who sat with an ice pack on her head.

"I'm fine, Morgan. Remember, it takes a lot to hurt a toy elephant."

"Yes, of course, but your phone call sounded hysterical."

"I'm sorry about that, Morgan. I was just so caught up in the fact that once again my so-called state of grace cut me off from the needs and mayhem of the world and—"

"Hello, Mr.—?" The policeman stood beside Morgan, holding a notepad.

"Johansson."

"Mr. Johansson, is this your elephant?"

"Mr. Emmanuelle lives with me."

"So he's your elephant."

Morgan bristled. "Mr. Emmanuelle belongs to no one. He is his own elephant. He shares my apartment."

"Uh-huh." The policeman made notes. Morgan clenched his fists.

"And do you know an Emma Louise Smolinsky?"

"WHO?!" Morgan and I shouted simultaneously. I, however, added to the moment by toppling quickly off the table and onto the floor, where I bounced slightly and came to rest. "WHO?" I shouted again, righting myself.

"Emma Louise Smolinsky," the detective said to me. Then turning to Morgan, "I gather she is familiar to you."

"Nathan, isn't that the name—"

"Mr. Johansson, I am speaking to you. I will get the elephant's statement later."

"No. I have no current knowledge of an Emma Louise Smolinsky," Morgan said through gritted teeth.

"But how do you know her name, Detective?" I asked.

"Luggage tags," he said briefly to me. I could tell that he held toy elephants in very low regard, but it didn't matter to me. I trotted over to the luggage, which I had not even noticed before.

"And there would be no particular reason then for her coming to see you," said the detective to Morgan.

"Coming to see me?" Morgan turned on me suddenly. "Nathan, what have you done?"

"Nothing! Honestly, Morgan. This time nothing but write a few opening sentences, order a salami on a baguette and a glass of a somewhat winsome Pinot Grigio, begin an intriguing conversation with a slumped-over young woman, and arrive too late to save her from two burly beasts who shoved her into a car with diplomatic plates."

"With what?" asked the detective.

"Oh, and I bought this beret."

"With diplomatic plates?" asked the detective.

"I see," said Morgan, sitting down and sipping absently at my remaining Pinot Grigio. "It *is* winsome," he mused.

"Perfect for lunch," I said, "when you want something light yet—"

"Is this your card, sir?"

Morgan looked at the proffered business card.

"Yes it is," he said, looking at me a bit darkly.

"And this is your note on the back?"

Morgan turned the card over. It said, "Thank you for a wonderful time." He looked at me a bit more darkly. "No, it is not my note on the back."

"Oh really?"

"Really. I am not in the habit of thanking myself for a good time. But I understand if you need a lie detector test and handwriting analysis to try and prove me wrong."

It truly amazed me how much Morgan could say through gritted teeth. If he wasn't already doing so well as a teacher and mentor, I might have suggested he take up ventriloquism.

"Detective, isn't it possible that it could be Emma Louise's own writing?" I asked, trying to defuse a situation which I was, after all, completely responsible for. Once again.

"Yeah. I guess," the detective said grudgingly. But where'd she get the card?

Morgan looked at me.

"Oh. Well. I—it seems . . . I mean . . . Well, the fact is I gave it to her."

"Why?"

"She asked for it."

"Why?"

"I'm guessing so she could write on the back. For in truth, we did have a lovely time together, and it turns out we both love tiramisu."

"Okay. But that still doesn't explain why I got such a stereophonic response when I said her name."

"That can be easily explained," Morgan said suavely.

"I'm waiting."

"My mother's name was Emma Louise Smolinksy. And I—we haven't heard that name in years. The fact is she passed about twenty years ago—a dreadful accident at the Omaha marketplace. Even at this late date, I find it almost impossible to talk about."

Even after all the theater I had seen, I was still astonished at how some people could lie so truthfully. Even knowing it was Morgan's profession, I actually found myself getting a bit teary.

The detective, whose success was dependent on seeing through people's lies, looked at Morgan for a full minute. Morgan held his gaze, sniffling slightly.

"You said you had no knowledge of—"

"I said *current knowledge*," corrected Morgan.

"Don't leave town," the detective said.

"Oh, Nathan! Remind me to cancel those airplane tickets to Monte Carlo," Morgan called loudly as we exited the café.

"Morgan, you should maybe try and get that bristling under control," I said gently as we headed home—myself stuffed in a jacket pocket, Morgan carrying my present after promising several times not to look inside the bag.

After a block or two of silent thought, I asked, "Morgan, do you think it's possible?"

Morgan looked at me kindly. "Of course it is possible."

"She did seem surprised about the *Christ* part. Although everyone was when they heard it. Perhaps she didn't recognize me because of her sluggish state, the dim light, and this ridiculous beret."

"The beret is a lovely touch, Nathan. You mustn't scold yourself about the beret."

"It brought me nothing but trouble. It made me irritable, deaf, and unrecognizable. That's what I get for trying to look like an artiste."

"There's probably a lesson here, Nathan, but we're exhausted. We'll be able to see everything a lot more clearly in the morning."

"Morgan. Perhaps she did recognize me and decided to keep it to herself."

"Perhaps," Morgan agreed.

"But why?" I asked.

"I don't know, pal. That's why we have the future."

"Ah!" I said, oddly comforted. We slowly made our way upstairs. It was about ten o'clock, and we were both looking forward to a cup of tea and a few poems before bed. Thankfully, it was impossible that the day could hold further adventure.

You can imagine my consternation when, as we rounded our last flight of stairs, we found Sadie sleeping quietly at our front door, nestled amidst her shopping bags and clutching her script to her chest as Elvis guarded her, much as the Aku-Akus did on Easter Island.

Morgan turned to look at me. I thought to run, but honestly, where would I have gone?

The Packaged Deal

The next morning found the three of us rumpled and a bit befuddled, gathering our wits over fresh Panama Esmerelda Gesha coffee, savoring its notes of bergamot and jasmine as well as its delicately structured ripe acidity.

"My *goodness*, this is good coffee!" said Sadie, gathering an afghan about her. "And I wouldn't know a note of bergamot if I tripped over it. When I think of the limitations that one gathers, *unknowingly*, through the years." She shook her head in amazement. "One day you look up and you see yourself surrounded by the same items in your pantry that you have bought for *thirty years*. Have I ever thought to buy anything other than Folgers? Well, sure, if there was a sale, as sometimes there is and some can is mysteriously thirty cents cheaper or whatever . . . but to decide on—" And here she picked up the bag and read the label carefully, "Pan-a-ma Es-mer-el-da Ge-sha. Well, I feel I would have had to have lived a different life entirely."

Both Morgan and I nodded silently, for while we could not exactly understand where this thread was leading, we both understood that it was heartfelt. Also, we both needed to warm up to the day, to speech, to thought, and consequently usually found ourselves at a coffee shop, letting its jangling silverware and sweet waitresses, sharp arcs of sunlight, and brisk currents of air passing to and fro the open door woo us to full awakening.

"I can remember the day I decided to buy Toilet Duck! I mean I actually felt adventurous about it!" And suddenly she lowered her voice. "And do you know I actually felt *furtive*? As if I was betraying Mr. Clean? Can you imagine? *I mean can you imagine?*"

I still felt a bit out of my league.

"I mean I suppose you both eat all sorts of exotic foodstuffs, don't you?"

"Well, yes actually," I said, although very little came out. I cleared my throat and tried again. "Well, yes, actually we do. We go out or order from various different restaurants many nights: Japanese, Uzbekistan, Chinese, Thai, Ukrainian, Italian." And here I stopped, for I was remembering the delightful little Italian pastries, flakey shells filled with a sweet cream, and I realized it had been a very long time since my salami sandwich.

"That's one of the many lovely things about New York—all the differences. All the *passionate* differences." Sadie gazed out the window a moment. "After the show, everyone went to Good Time Charley's, you know, because it was a packaged deal: bus, lunch, show, dinner. And I got in there, you know, the long tables all prepared for this big group of senior citizens, the pitchers of sangria, the salads all made and sitting on the plate, everything done so we would get our money's worth and be as little bother to them as possible and I don't know . . . I approached a seat, and I just saw that salad sitting there. I saw that lettuce—lettuce that I think I've seen practically every day of my adult life. You know, those salads you get at weddings in plastic wooden bowls, layers of limp lettuce, one slide of tomato, a bit of red onion, a dollop of Russian dressing, and I just panicked. It suddenly mattered to me terribly that I didn't matter to whoever made that salad—that I was supposed to just sit down and chew on all that roughage and chatter away and not notice, not care about the prodigious sameness.

"Do you know we have a Good Time Charley's back home? In the mall? And I realized we had come to New York City and done everything we could *not* to come to New York City. And I just felt suddenly that I had, in a way, lived my life so as *not* to live my life. And I knew I would not be able to face the prime rib and baked potato and cheesecake that were coming, and everything got so eerie and strange, and everyone looked like horses at their feed bags and there was snorting and hooves. I swear I could hear snorting and hooves, and I got hot and cold and I excused myself and said, 'I really must go.' And I grabbed my earthly goods, as it were, and ran out onto the street and do you know *not one of the group came out to get me and urge me back inside?* But at the same time, this made a lot of sense to me because why would a horse do that?

"And there I was out on the street, alone for the first time in my life because—I don't know if Nathan shared this with you, Morgan, but my husband recently left me for a younger woman."

Morgan looked at me astonished.

"Morgan, it was late and there is only so much one day can handle," I said. And he nodded, remembering yesterday and all that had occurred.

"So there I was, out on some corner of New York City, a city I— well, all of us I suppose, on the bus trip—had been taught to be so terrified of that we would go only if it resembled our mall back home. And it was about six now, rush hour, and I didn't know what to do. I didn't know what to *do!*

"And suddenly, this very gentle black man, *African American* man I mean. His coat was ragged and he had slipped his feet into his shoes so his heels were exposed. They were probably not even his shoes, and he had this knit Giants football cap on. You know, with a large pom-pom. He had a beard, and he was stooped over a bit. I mean he had to shuffle, and I thought, *Oh my god! On top of everything else, this man is going to rob me.* And I thought, *Just give him the lamp. Maybe he'll leave you alone if you give him the lamp.* So I held out the lamp, and he took my arm—do you know, I don't think I have ever been actually touched by a black man? And he hailed a cab for me and put me in! I swear I would not have been able to hail a cab, that's how paralyzed I had become! And he gave the cab driver money—two twenties, I think. This very poor black man who looked like he begged all day. He gave the cabdriver money and said, 'Take her wherever she needs to go.' And I had your card, and believe it or not, I felt so safe when I got here—even though, of course, I had to stay out in the hallway, just having my head against your door, Nathan. And Morgan, of course," she added hurriedly. "I just felt so safe that I fell into a profound sleep without even taking the sleeping pills that my doctor had prescribed since John left. I slept like a baby."

Morgan nodded. He seemed lost in thought. I was sure I was going to feel his penetrating and icy blue stare upon me, for how would Sadie have known to come here if I hadn't been incontinent once again with Morgan's business card? Thankfully, he remained lost in thought.

"I know, I know. I should do the right thing and commit myself somewhere," said Sadie tiredly.

"Meaning?" asked Morgan.

"Well, meaning I'm crazy," said Sadie very matter-of-factly. (Exceedingly matter-of-factly, given the sentiment.) "I mean I am."

"Really?"

"Well, of course I am! Did you just hear all I said? Horses and feedbags and hooves and pom-poms. I mean if I didn't think I was crazy, I'd be—" And here she stopped suddenly, her face transforming from a vacant sadness to a kind of vigor as she brought herself to the close of a seeming conundrum. "Why . . . I'd be crazy."

"Yes," said Morgan.

"Just a minute," I said, hoping I was following. "You mean by virtue of the fact that Sadie thinks she's crazy, she probably isn't?"

"Well, I am not a therapist by any means, even though my job sometimes spills into that area occasionally. For artists are on thin ice, make no mistake. Very thin ice, and so, of course, if you have any doubts, I urge you to visit the therapist or asylum of your choice. And I mean that with deep respect. But from where I sit, Sadie, you are on a mythic journey."

"My god," I said, awed.

"You've left the known world of the packaged deal, for it had become terrifying to see yourself chomping at the feed bag of life, as it were, and you ran. You met a gentle guide in the most unlikely of circumstances, and he helped you across the river. And here you are."

"But it is so extreme," said Sadie.

"Yes, but you've had an extreme life, Sadie."

"So you don't think I need to commit myself?" she asked in a small and hopeful voice.

"Oh yes, definitely commit yourself," said Morgan. "But commit yourself to *yourself*."

"Oh my *god*," said Sadie in awe.

"Now excuse me for just one moment," said Morgan. And he left the room. In a few moments, we could hear him typing on his computer, no doubt having had—as is his wont—a thought.

Sadie straightened up the couch and folded the afghan, brushed her hair, and gathered her belongings. I mused on how good a couple of eggs over easy with crisp bacon would go right about now and wondered if Morgan would have time or if he had a morning class at the Academy. A message started clicking its way on the machine.

"Morgan? Hi, it's me, Cheryl? You remember from the other night? Cookie suggested I give you a call? Because Arnold is doing this Shakespearean show? And Cookie thought I would be good as part of *Midsummer*. Which I don't understand, but I trust her. Anyway, I wondered if you had any time. I'm at the health club right now, and you can call me here. I would really appreciate it. Thank you, bye."

The machine clicked again.

"Morgan? Jason a.k.a. Supalady. I have a shot at *X-files*. Can you believe it? *I* mean *can you believe it?* A drag queen makes it to prime time? Pinch me! Couldn't wait until I see you at class this morning to tell you."

The machine clicked again.

"Morgan, it's Sal. They're calling me back for *All My Children*. Thank you so much. Can I come in tonight, tomorrow, whenever? I know it's short notice, but it is really important."

"*All My Children*! Oh my god!" said Sadie. "I wonder if he's the new Kurt!"

The machine clicked.

"Morgan? It's me, Cheryl? Hi, you remember from the other night? I just left a message? I asked you to call me, but I didn't leave my phone number. I'm such a dork! Anyway, just dial MUS-CLES. Thanks!"

Morgan came out of the bedroom.

"Ready for some bacon and eggs?" he asked.

"Morgan, you've got a morning class," I said, feeling the depressing need to be responsible.

"All the more reason to avail ourselves of the Cholesterol Special. Sadie, will you join us?"

"No thank you, Morgan. I need to get back because I have a couple of things I need to do back home. I would love, however, to leave my script here, if you have the time."

"Of course," said Morgan.

"And what are you going to do back home, Sadie?" I asked, perhaps impertinently, but wanting desperately to know if she was, indeed, going to commit herself to an asylum.

Sadie looked up and gazed out the window. We could just see the tip of the Empire State Building.

"I am going to take him for everything he's got."

"Excellent. And might I suggest you peruse this volume, if you like, on your bus journey home," said Morgan, giving her his thoroughly read copy of *Myths to Live By*, by the superb Joseph Campbell. "You might wish to begin with chapter 10."

"Oh, how kind of you! I will definitely return it when I am finished."

"No need. I have several. Pass it on."

Indeed, dear reader, Sadie herself suddenly seemed a younger woman.

In a matter of moments, we had escorted Sadie to a cab, waved our good-byes, then waved our hellos as we entered our Studio Coffee

Shoppe—I musing on how quickly life can be a series of hellos and good-byes with worlds colliding and transforming in between. Sadie had asked us to keep the Elvis lamp, as a promise of her return, and the three of us settled in our booth.

After we placed our order, Morgan reached into his pocket and pulled out an envelope.

"For you, Nathan."

I was stunned, for what could there be for me so early in the morning? I opened the envelope and, dear reader, while I understood the practicalities behind what Morgan had done, my heart soared with a sudden sense of belonging, a sense I hadn't known since the days of tea beneath the willow tree with Emma Louise. For there in the envelope were twenty-five business cards similar to Morgan's in regard to pertinent information, but for the following:

NATHAN EMMANUELLE
AUTHOR IN THE MAKING

From Bard to Verse

While I like to think I have become something of an experienced theatergoer, having now had the opportunity to attend all manner of productions, from the decorous and vaulting heights of Broadway houses to tiny black box theaters fueled only by the unbounded hopes and dreams of youth, this was the first evening where we entered a theater and were greeted by a priest. He stood ready with a warm handshake and a chuckle for each of us as we entered. He put me very much in mind of the character of Don Camillo, magnificently realized by the superb writer Giovannino Guareschi—except, of course, that Don Camillo was a bit of a hothead, big and strong with hard fists, and the priest we had just met was small, round, and genial.

"Good lord!" said Morgan aptly, settling himself into his chair, visibly shaken from the encounter.

"How unexpected!" I said. "How startling and yet how comforting."

"Comforting!" Morgan snorted, looking around at the audience and unwrapping his scarf while putting his hat under his chair, unbuttoning his sport coat, and scanning the program, seemingly all in one smooth motion.

"Yes. One simply does not expect a man of the cloth to have a foot planted so enthusiastically in a part of life which historically has so often been on the fringes of correct society."

"Oh. *Society*." Morgan snorted again.

I had never heard Morgan snort in such quick succession and immediately surmised something was amiss. For Morgan was too much a man of reflexive generosity—a man for whom the present moment was always new, fresh, innocent, untainted by history. And so to hear him pass such dreadful judgment on the priesthood and society was too uncharacteristic.

Morgan looked again abstractly at the house. I noted a faint whiff of incense in the air, perhaps the sweet remnant of a morning mass from upstairs, and suddenly felt a sleepy peace wash over me. And as Morgan perused his program, I closed my eyes and was briefly, eerily transported to Bristol's St. Mary's Church—to a soft "Tantum Ergo Sacramentum," to vaulting stone walls and brilliant stained-glass windows casting soft pastel patterns on draped statuary, and to the strong pudgy clutch of a child's arm.

"Dominus nobiscum," I murmured unaccountably.

"Et cum spirit tu tuo," responded Morgan automatically.

We looked at each other in astonishment.

"I was an altar boy," said Morgan. "And yourself?"

"I don't know," I said, puzzled. "Suddenly, I was there at St. Mary's." I elucidated the memories of the above paragraph, ending with a catch in my throat as I said, "With a strong pudgy arm clutching me."

"Emma Louise?" suggested Morgan gently.

"Probably. I do seem to remember she would insist on taking me to mass. How good of her to insist on my getting a sound basis in the abstract notions of religion and worship."

"Especially as she was probably all of three or four at the time," agreed Morgan.

"Indeed." There was a brief pause as we contrived to fold ourselves up enough to let some large people pass in front of us, looking for their seats. Suddenly, a thought occurred to me. "Did you say you were an altar boy?" I queried, my astonishment loud in the murmuring house.

"Yes. Many of us were."

"Did you ever want to become a priest?"

Morgan hesitated, his eyes seeing something far away, maybe something lost.

"Yes, very much. For one summer, anyway."

"Oh, you would have made an excellent priest, Morgan. Perhaps your past life continues in the present, for in some ways, you comport yourself as one even now."

"Oh really!" Morgan snorted. He looked around. And then I suddenly realized the cause of his snorting, his anxiety, his ungenerous thoughts toward society and the priesthood.

"Is she here?" I asked.

"Who?" asked Morgan innocently.

Having recently experienced his brilliant impromptu performance on his mother's name and demise, I now gave him what was for me a knowing look.

"No," said Morgan wistfully.

Suddenly, the house and stage lights went out. A startling cacophony of sound erupted. Blue lights rose on the stage; fog streamed forth. A harsh blare of thunder—sharp white light. Rough-hewn creatures lumbered from the audience, screaming and cackling and rolling themselves about on stage. All were dressed in what looked like masses of seaweed, great ugly dripping creatures, but each wearing the compelling adornment of a crisp white chef's hat. They began the witches' scene from the Scottish Play while methodically creating what looked like a startlingly good boeuf bourguignon in their giant saucepan. They came down to the foot of the stage, staring at us vigorously as if to say "If you even *think* about lifting the lid and sampling the concoction, you will be part of the dinner." The point tacitly made, they rolled away.

Suddenly, "You Must Have Been a Beautiful Baby" started to play from a rinky-dink piano; and when the singer began, we recognized Evelyn's husky alto voice. A tall young man, dressed in the gracious summer suit of 1912 with straw bowler, came running helter-skelter down the aisle carrying a lawn chair and implored a gentleman in the first row to give up his seat in exchange. The gentleman did so good-naturedly, whereupon the desperate young man took his seat, pretended to be a member of the audience, and started to read the program.

Suddenly a tall gawky girl—her hair askew, her sailor middy muddy and torn—came running on stage and, seeing the young gentleman sitting in the audience, screeched "LYSANDER!" and leapt into his lap, punching and biting him. He stood, deposited her into the lap of the gentleman who had graciously given up his seat, and beat a hasty exit back up the aisle, the gawky girl following, screaming her lines in perfect iambic pentameter.

As our attention was turned to the back of the theater, a man in a costume of patched-together elements of uniforms through the ages entered reading a letter, followed by Cookie who was attired purely and quite becomingly, in a sheet. Morgan tensed and held his breath. He had confided in me that for all her strong positive energy, she was probably in way over her head.

She began simply and honestly. When she parted the sheet and "cut" her thigh, there was a gasp from the audience and from myself as well, even though I knew it was lipstick.

Then the duke in *Measure for Measure* demanded Isabel become his wife, and when the retinue left joyously to prepare for the coming nuptials, Isabel, alone in a shocked silence, staggered off, sobbing that her future had been wrested from her without so much as a by-your-leave. But without so much as a by-your-leave! I would have sobbed as well.

And so the evening continued in this way, the audience careening from one time period to the next, from one madcap or tragic crisis to another, barely able to catch our collective breath—Arnold having timed the scenes so perfectly that the audience never had enough time to clap and thereby shake off their increasingly pent-up energy.

Suddenly, just when we felt we were too exhausted from the rawness of emotion, the sheer physicality of the evening, actors ran briskly around the room passing out Danishes.

"Oh no," said Morgan. "He *wouldn't.*"

I was just about to ask Morgan who *he* was and what he wouldn't do when a sharp cold white spotlight revealed the back of a black-clothed young man, and I realized we were suddenly guests of the quintessentially dysfunctional Hamlet family, dining metaphorically on the thrifty funeral meats.

Suddenly the young man turned, enraged, and began, "Now I am alone! O, what a rogue and peasant slave am I!" The force and passion and presence of the actor would have been extraordinary enough, but what made it infinitely more so was that the actor was Abby.

* * *

Needless to say, the applause on the curtain call was hearty and enthusiastic as the ten actors, all in varying costumes, reminded us of the broad range of topography and history we had covered while visiting with the Great Bard.

In the press of the exiting theater patrons, Arnold was quick to make his way through to Morgan much as an announcer would to a coach of a winning football team. "Mr. Johansson! Mr. Johansson! Thank you so much for coming! Nathan! Great to see you!" Arnold was as enthusiastic and rumpled as ever.

"Exceptional work, Arnold," said Morgan.

"Oh. I just kind of let them go," said Arnold bashfully.

"No, truly, Arnold. It was outstanding. I do not say these things lightly. I barely say them at all."

"He is correct, Arnold," I concurred. "I have only ever heard him use the word *exceptional* once, and it had to do with a tenderloin at Delmonico's."

"Oh my god," said Arnold, now understanding the import of Morgan's statements. "Oh, Mr. Johansson, I would like you to meet Father O'Malley."

Morgan shook hands with the small, round, and cherubic priest.

"Weren't they astounding!" Father O'Malley said.

"Thanks, Father," said Arnold. "We are incredibly indebted to Father O'Malley for he gives us this space for free."

"Not for free, Arnold," the priest remonstrated sternly but with a twinkle in his eye.

"You got me there, Father!" Arnold grinned good-naturedly. "We have to pay for the space." But on the world *pay*, Arnold made the characteristic finger quote gesture, as if to indicate that he didn't consider it a "payment" at all. "How we 'pay' our rent is we have to perform two miracle plays—one at Christmas, the other at Easter." Arnold added unnecessarily, "In other words, we 'pay' to perform by *performing*!"

And indeed, no businessman could have exhibited more pride in snaring a multimillion dollar account than did Arnold in this moment.

"That is a generous agreement, Father," Morgan said politely. "An exchange which benefits all parties considerably."

"MORGAN! MORGAN!" Cookie called from the stage and then threw herself into Morgan's arms. I must say I was not the only one who envied Morgan his unexpected package of femininity wrapped in 100 percent percale. "Was the blood believable?" she asked anxiously.

"The blood was believable, and so was your work. Truly wonderful."

"Oh! Hello, Father!" said Cookie, attempting to regain her composure as best one can when one is very beautiful, flushed with victory, and slipping out of a sheet.

"MORGAN! MORGAN!" Cheryl called from the stage, running and then throwing herself into Morgan's arms. "How did I do?" For indeed, it was *Cheryl* who had rushed onstage in a state of muddy and torn dishabille, throwing herself courageously into Lysander's lap!

"My goodness! Cheryl! I didn't even *recognize* you!" said Morgan, shocked.

"That is a majorly huge compliment, Cheryl," said Cookie knowingly. "It means you were like totally consumed by your character, such that your actual self was *obliterated*."

"Is that good?" Cheryl asked in a small voice.

"My god, Cheryl, it's like devoutly to be wished!" Cookie hugged Cheryl in congratulations.

"Hi, Father!" said Cheryl, still beaming from having obliterated herself.

"How blessed we are to have two such brilliant and beautiful women gracing our stage at St. Bernard's. Cheryl, it was astonishing to me that Lysander didn't want to marry you *instantly*! And, Cookie, I think we all understood tonight what an actual brute Brutus could be."

Cookie was astonished. "Father, I never thought of that before!"

"That is completely brilliant!" said Cheryl.

"Do you think *Shakespeare* even knew he had been that brilliant?" asked Cookie, hooking her arm into one of the priest's while Cheryl did the same on the other side, escorting him backstage to the opening night festivities.

There was a moment of brief but tangible appreciation in Morgan's eye for the padre, and I marveled again that when life happens in an unguarded moment before history and preconceived notions arrive to insulate you in the sameness of your being, you step forward into new places in your own soul.

"He's a likeable guy," I offered.

"He's a very likeable guy," Morgan answered.

"Maybe we'll start attending mass now," I suggested, thinking happily of soaring architecture, candles, and choral odes.

"Don't push it."

"Right," I said quickly.

Morgan turned to Arnold. "Arnold, again I have to say what a directorial accomplishment this was, for in fact, I did coach Cheryl a bit on the scene. But you took her to new heights with your astonishing insouciance."

"Gosh, Mr. Johansson, that means a lot coming from you. Besides which, to be honest, I have never heard the word 'insouciance' before. It would also mean a lot to the company if you would just come back and, you know, say basically 'hi' or words to that effect," said Arnold, leading Morgan by the arm.

I marveled how Arnold, in his gently half-crazed and rumpled way, managed so adroitly to coalesce all the right people at exactly the right time.

And in the frenzied rush, Morgan and I were whirled into the backstage ebullience of a solid opening night. Champagne was poured, toasts were made, and cannoli was passed about. Suddenly, Morgan caught sight of Abby pressed against an exit door by Jeremy, who was gesticulating in what can only be described an angry and arrogant fashion. Finally, Jeremy took Abby's arm and propelled her out the door, seemingly against her will.

Morgan, seeing this, and being a gentleman who has in the past saved two people from knife fights, run after a dazed child in the middle of Thirty-Fourth Street, and performed CPR on his neighbor when he was found unconscious in the hallway, instantly tried to—

("NATHAN!" Morgan said sternly on reading my work. "Delete these details *right now!*")

"Morgan, I cannot and will not," I said just as sternly. "For how do I evoke the true heroics of our time if I do not continue to represent the darkness that always threatens to overtake us? How will this chronicle serve to inspire an understanding that a better life comes through attention to details both large and small, to vigilance, to the pursuit of virtue, if we come off merely as a couple of bon vivants in silk scarves who have no relevance because we did not, on occasion, also take courage in both hands and step into the deep wells of despair, darkness, and cruelty?"

At this, Morgan was—for one of the few times in his life—silenced.

And I think, dear reader, we may have dispensed once and for all with Morgan's reticence vis à vis the personal details of his life.

For I have come to understand that my mentor—along with being an infinite wellspring of generosity and courage—has, in his very own center, the same dark demons that hover on the sidewalks of this great city. In this, we are all microcosms of our universe. And in this large swing between our own demonic and godlike energies, we mirror the creation and crumbling of great civilizations: the holocausts, the redemptions, the man who builds the gas chamber, and the woman who keeps her neighbors safe through the terror. In our darkest night, it is not that we are afraid that God does not exist, or that he exists only to judge us and relegate us to perdition. Our greatest fear is that God is just like us. What then awaits us in the afterlife? At best, an infinite tussle with our almighty selves.

But I digress.

Morgan, upon seeing this, instantly tried to make his way toward Abby. Were it not for the crowd, Morgan would have flattened Jeremy, become bruised himself, and would have had to deal with the police which, you may recall, is not the most graceful of Morgan's attributes.

Perhaps it was the effect of the champagne and the dizzying and boundless energy packed to the point of explosion in the cramped area of the backstage, or most likely it was the emotional distraction that Abby's exit affected, but when Arnold asked if Morgan would be on the board of directors, Morgan said yes without thinking, his eyes still burning holes in the large steel fire door as if to eviscerate Jeremy once and for all.

And when Arnold managed to quiet everyone down to make the announcement, no one looked more surprised than Morgan himself.

The Venn Diagram

"I REALLY WANT TO THANK YOU FOR THIS, MORGAN!" shouted Arnold as the map of Connecticut slapped back and forth against us, catching the currents of the wind which roared about us in our perky little midnight-blue Subaru convertible with cream interior, for Morgan was speeding along at a solid sixty-seven miles per hour, his former trepidation forgotten, a mighty sense of power now coursing through his being as he bore down firmly onto the accelerator pedal.

"YOU'RE WELCOME, ARNOLD. NATHAN AND I WERE LOOKING FORWARD TO A FOLIAGE TOUR IN NEW ENGLAND, ANYWAY," responded Morgan. "TELL ME WHAT WE ARE LOOKING FOR."

"COUNTY ROAD 515." The map slapped Arnold in the head. "OR 29. OR 17. OR A SIGN FOR PORKER'S CORNERS."

"OKAY!" roared Morgan. "IT'S GOOD TO HAVE SOME LEEWAY."

We were packed for a weekend trip to Porker's Corners, where we would leave Arnold to his family responsibilities and then browse about the countryside, looking at foliage and antiques. We had packed small overnight bags as well as the Elvis head, since Arnold had been so transfixed by it this morning and Morgan was more than grateful to pass it along.

I was propped in the center between pilot and navigator, my only job to sit on the lid of a picnic basket that had been lovingly packed by Cookie for our trip. I was suddenly reminded of darling Nancy Drew:

> "As Nancy expertly backed her roadster out of the beautifully winding drive, Hannah Gruen, the kindly old housekeeper who had taken care of Nancy since her mother's death so many years ago, came running from the palatial home surrounded by ancient oaks and maples with a picnic hamper she had lovingly packed with sandwiches, lemonade, and her special Wacky Cake.
>
> "Stop, Nancy!" called Bess, Nancy's chubby chum. "Here comes Hannah and I think she has a hamper packed with wonderful food!"
>
> "Hooray! Hooray!" said the rest of the chums, knowing that now they would have a solid luncheon filled with tasty nutrition before venturing further onto the grim and decaying estate to hunt for the old clock that Mr. Larson said would reveal the secrets of Aunt Eloise's mysteriously missing will."

I thought about my opening sentences, penned not so long ago at that very eventful afternoon at Café Des Artistes, and felt they simply could not hold a candle to those penned by Carolyn Keene so many years ago. How then does a writer continue, knowing that so much good work has already been done, work that one cannot ever hope to match? It was a disquieting thought for I had decided it was to be my life's work. If I did not have my writing, what could I possibly choose instead?

I made my mind turn to the contents of the picnic basket, for though I did not know what was in it, I knew it would be delicious as Cookie had shown a remarkable propensity for the culinary arts. She had also shown a remarkable propensity for Arnold, which surprised me very much as I had imagined Cookie and Morgan would be "an item." I was chastened by the fact that life's plotlines were often so much more interesting than my own, but then reminded myself that life had been at the business far longer than myself.

Another convertible passed us on the left, filled with a bevy of beautiful babes. They honked the car horn and waved, white teeth shining, arms waving, their heads of long hair—ash and chestnut and strawberry blond—forming a huge cloud of tangles as they whipped past us in the brilliant autumn sunlight. We waved and watched in a kind of reverence.

"MORGAN, CAN I ASK YOUR ADVICE?" shouted Arnold.

"SURE, ARNOLD," shouted Morgan jauntily. I could tell he loved the speed, the sun, the unexpected glimpses of feminine beauty, the foliage. No doubt he felt the advice would have something to do with choosing between 519 or 29 or a sign for Porker's Corners. "SHOOT!" he added happily in an uncharacteristic vernacular.

"COOKIE AND I HAVE GOTTEN REALLY CLOSE, BUT I WANTED TO SAVE SEX FOR AFTER MARRIAGE BUT I'M THIRTY-FIVE AND SUDDENLY NOT SURE."

Morgan careened sharply onto the shoulder and suddenly hit the brakes. I was thankful both Morgan and Arnold had used their seat belts and that I had thought to wedge myself under the handle of the picnic basket. We took a moment to catch our breaths and let the sudden silence settle in our ears.

"Excuse me?" said Morgan.

"Cookie and I have gotten really close, but I wanted to save sex for after marriage but I'm thirty-five, and I'm suddenly not sure."

"Uh-huh," said Morgan quietly. "And why are you no longer sure, Arnold?" asked Morgan adroitly, stalling for time while seeming not to.

I, for one, wanted to ask what Arnold was no longer sure about since it seemed that it could be so many things. Maybe he was no longer sure he was thirty-five, for instance.

"I don't know exactly. She wants it and—"

"And?"

"And I . . . I guess I want it. But I really believe it's, you know, important."

"Uh-huh."

"And it's worth waiting for and all. But I guess I'm a bit of an anomaly. And I've lost some terrific women, I think, because of it. I mean, you know, losing Abby. That was tough. I mean she would get really . . . I mean late at night for instance, she would—"

"All that is water under the bridge," said Morgan quickly. "The point is you must do what you think is right, Arnold. And what you think is right can, of course, change. What you had determined to do at the age of twenty may no longer be right for you now. It doesn't mean you were wrong then or that you are wrong now. It simply means you have changed now and the act of making love is understood as an expression of deep feeling. That expression won't be any less special after marriage—not any less special than if, for instance, Cookie had decided not to pack a picnic basket until after you were married. Think how we all would have been less for that!"

But then, as if Morgan suddenly realized the potentially disastrous metaphorical connotations implied by all of us sharing in Cookie's picnic basket, he added hurriedly, "I am certain there is a much better analogy than the picnic basket, Arnold, but you get the point here."

"Yeah," said Arnold, staring out at a brilliant red maple. "Yeah, I sure do, Morgan. Thanks so much. Gosh. You really put things in a great perspective. It's the kind of thing maybe I could have asked my dad or my older brother. But I don't have a brother, and my dad . . . well." In an uncharacteristic way, Arnold was suddenly silent

"Right. Well. Why don't we take this next turn for this state park and have at said picnic basket?" suggested Morgan.

"Okay," said Arnold, but I could tell he was not his usual ebullient self.

Morgan expertly steered the sport Subaru into a small parking lot framed by ancient oaks and maples, and we bounded off to the nearest picnic table to arrange the wonderfully varied array of foodstuffs.

As he did so, I rather nonchalantly (I see now in retrospect) bit into a hard-boiled egg and, dear reader, I was suddenly assaulted by the vibrant memory of a summer day, a similar picnic table, cars swishing by, and dear Emmet smiling with his darling daughter Emma Louise, the two of them racing down a large hill as sweet Elvira unpacked a luncheon and put a hard-boiled egg on a napkin for me as per Emma Louise's instructions. The wash of memory was so strong, so sweet, so unexpected, that I sat stone-still and staring, for in my subsequent history I had had no occasion to bite into another hard-boiled egg. And thus this recollection had lain locked inside, undiminished by time and remembrance. Morgan and Arnold did not notice my paralysis immediately as they were still in the thick of relationship matters.

"You know, Arnold, it is not for me to say, of course—but clearly, Cookie has very strong feelings for you. I mean look at the attention to detail that this lovely repast would indicate."

"Yeah," said Arnold distractedly. "I mean she knows I love Halloween and so she even packed these napkins with jack-o-lanterns on them.

And she knows I hate how sandwiches get soggy, so she kept the tomato slices separate."

"There has clearly been some emotional intimacy already."

"Yeah. Yeah, I know where you're going with this, Morgan. There has already been major intimacy, so why not—"

"Well, whatever. You know your own timing and so on."

"I just . . . The thing is . . . Oh hell." And Arnold drifted off.

I could see Emma Louise barreling down the slope with her fierce determination to beat her dad, and her dad good-naturedly slowing down (but not obviously) so that she would win. And then Emma stamped her foot. "You let me win!"

"No no no no no!" And Emmet laughed and scooped her up and put his arm around dear Elvira, and Emma picked me up by the ear and we were all clutched in a strong and familial embrace. So strong the memory! It seemed this hard-boiled egg so carefully swaddled in Saran Wrap by an ex-Rockette had become my madeleine.

"You okay, Nathan?" asked Morgan.

"Yes. Thank you. Yes."

"Really?"

"Yes. Yes, it's just the hard-boiled egg."

"Uh-huh," said Morgan helpfully.

But I had drifted off again.

"The truth is," Arnold continued. "The truth is that my dad. Well, he's crazy."

"Rest assured, Arnold, that one day you'll understand your father better. And the things he said and did and believed in will not seem quite so eccentric or rigid."

"No, I'm actually being literal. He's goes into an asylum on occasion. In fact, I'm bringing him the Elvis head since he was a fan once and I figured it would somehow maybe remind him of something. Sanity, perhaps."

"Oh."

"But the point is, I'm pretty sure I'll be crazy too someday."

"Ah."

"And I don't think I should ever have kids."

"And that's why you're not having sex?"

"Well, there's a connection, right?"

"Neither of us can know what caused your father's insanity. But you know what concerns me most, Arnold?" asked Morgan while tucking into the potato salad. "What concerns me most is when exactly are you going to tell your beloved your concerns? After you're married? Is the plan to lure her into a marriage and then tell her you might be carrying a crazy gene or something?"

"Gosh, that would be awful! Is that what I'm doing?"

"No."

"No?" And Arnold leaned forward with the same spellbinding sense that I had known however long ago when I had almost stepped into my saucer.

"I think not. I think what you are doing instead is making sure no woman ever gets to know that. I think you short-circuit the whole thing from the get-go by stopping the relationship at a point when you know the woman has no choice but to leave."

"Huh."

"There may be no crazy gene. And there may. But the point is Cookie may not even want children. Or she may want you more. The problem with such candor, of course, is that you would have to actually step into the pool of intimacy. And perhaps that is what you are avoiding."

"Holy cow!" shouted Arnold, slapping his forehead in the characteristic gesture that needs no description here. "I think you have just shattered my vital lie!" continued Arnold, echoing the profound contribution dear Ernest Becker made with his riveting *Denial of Death.*

"Uh-huh," said Morgan carefully while adding tomato slices to three ham sandwiches and setting them out for all of us. The quietude was enormous, as quietude can only be when two out of three companions are lost to an inward journey, one reeling from all the force of *Á La Recherche Du Temps Perdu*, the other staggering under the sudden collapse of his *sui generis*. We ate the rest of our meal in silence, and if Morgan was musing about the composition of his own internal life, I hoped for his sake it was at least in English.

"How about some Wacky Cake and lemonade before we head on out to Porker's Corners?" boomed Morgan energetically, attempting to rouse his fallen comrades.

Elvira at last had hustled Emma Louise into the 1955 Chevy after she took one more run down the hill, clutching my young self, my ears flying in the wind. I gazed upon the memory with a fierce lump—as if in its remembrance I felt its promise, and in its promise I felt its loss. I shivered.

"Nathan!" said Morgan, suddenly concerned. "You looked peaked."

I didn't hear him. For I was remembering as Emma Louise stepped up into the capacious backseat of the Chevy that there was a little cooing baby in a basket behind the driver. Odd, to suddenly remember that baby. Why had I forgotten him? Clearly, he must have been Emma Louise's brother. But why had I no recollection of him? Certainly, there would have been sibling tussles; certainly, he would have found me and carried me about with a misplaced proprietorial air until at last dear Elvira crafted him his own elephant, perhaps made out of his own mattress ticking printed with toy soldiers and the like. I felt dizzy with memory and conjecture and wished suddenly that I had not partaken of the hard-boiled egg that had opened the door on a past that created far too many questions.

"Nathan!" shouted Morgan.

I jumped. Morgan looked suddenly terribly pale.

"Morgan, what is it?" I said, my sad musing on the past suddenly obliterated by my concern with the present.

"You okay, Morgan?" asked Arnold, himself suddenly jolted from the shards of his vital lie.

"Yes. Yes, I'm fine," said Morgan, suddenly lying down on his side of the picnic table.

Arnold and I looked at each other. While Morgan was prone—literally—to taking naps at odd times during the day by lying down in our parlor, he never had done so quite so publicly. We peered over the top of the table. Indeed, he seemed asleep. Neither Arnold nor I were certain what the proper etiquette was in a situation such as this. After all, Morgan had not only driven us here but had striven to keep the conversation going while giving solid advice on marriage and sexuality, as well as coordinating the details of a delicious repast. Suddenly, both Arnold and I felt guilty.

"That was inexcusable of me," whispered Arnold. "I had no right to lose myself in the maelstrom of sudden self-knowledge."

"Nor I in the thunderous onrush of a forgotten past."

"What should we do?"

"I don't know. He usually sleeps for about two minutes and then he's ready to go."

"Okay," said Arnold. "I've got a second hand. If after two minutes he hasn't stirred—"

"No need," said Morgan. "I'm not napping. I was so suddenly unnerved that I had to lie down and get my balance." He popped up. "I'm fine now."

"But what happened, Morgan? What unnerved you on this brilliant autumn afternoon?" I asked plaintively.

"Oh, it's silly really."

"Go ahead, Morgan," said Arnold. "After all, you've just learned my most intimate secret to date."

"And you know everything there is to know about me," I said. "More, probably."

Morgan looked at the innocent expectation that greeted him from across the table. A man never given to disclosure, but only to one of counseling and helping others, I wondered if he would take his own advice now and step into a pool of intimacy. We waited, both Arnold and myself uncharacteristically still, as if we recognized the largenes of such a step. Morgan shook his head in wonderment.

"It's just I seem to have had a vision."

"Yes?" I asked casually, deliberately helping myself to another piece of Wacky Cake so that Morgan would not become skittish and self-conscious. And to be completely honest, because the cake was very good.

"Well, I looked over at you, Nathan, and suddenly you were much larger, and I was actually looking up at you. And you—well, you were a toy." He shook his head and chuckled. "I mean a toy, you know. And you didn't speak, and I didn't speak, but I—" And here Morgan gazed forward into the vision again. "I reached for you, and you were suddenly just a toy. Just a toy. And it unnerved me to think that you could sit silent and still, just like a toy on a shelf and not—"

"And not like the somewhat demonically catalytic agent that I have been."

"Exactly." Morgan smiled.

The shadows had suddenly dramatically lengthened, and we were all silent. Then I asked, "Morgan, in your vision—"

"Yes?"

"In your vision, were you *cooing*?"

"Cooing?" And Morgan looked startled. "Cooing." He thought about it. "No. No, I can't say as I remember cooing."

"Uh-huh," I said, striving for calm. "But, Morgan, do you even know what cooing *is*?"

"Well." I could see Morgan begin to laugh as he tried to give my question respectful consideration.

And then Arnold put a napkin on his head to create a facsimile of a baby's sun bonnet. He let his eyes grow large and lose their focus and waved his arms in the soft, helpless way babies do and earnestly did a babylike cooing, all of which created an extraordinary transformation.

"That was excellent," I said.

"I had to play a baby in a melodrama once."

"Yes, it was truly well done, Arnold," said Morgan, ever one to give good notes whenever possible. "But no, I cannot say I remember"— and now Morgan began to allow the laughter to burble forth, thinking he would be able to communicate at the same time—"ever actually . . ." He caught his breath and clutched his sides; the laughter would simply not take second place to speech. "Coo—" His eyes began to tear. "Coo—" Valiantly he tried again, but it was hopeless. He was gone. He lay back down on the bench, out of our line of sight, large guffaws erupting from the other side of the table the only proof that he was still there.

Arnold and I looked at each other. I shrugged. What was there to do? We waited patiently for the laughter to subside.

"I set him off with that performance," Arnold said.

"Maybe." I nodded. "We'll give him a minute or two."

Eventually, Morgan quieted down (much to our relief), sat up, and wiped his eyes with the very napkin Arnold had used for his baby bonnet.

"Well! I'm exhausted!"

Indeed, it seemed that this innocent repast, meant only to strengthen us as we made our way to Porker's Corners, had in fact been an enormous journey unto itself.

We hustled our picnic detritus into the basket, ourselves into the Subaru, and returned once more to that infinite ribbon of highway.

As Arnold and Morgan began singing "This Land Is Your Land," I peered, with some trepidation, into the backseat, but all that greeted me was the Elvis head. I wasn't certain if the intensity of my feeling meant I was disappointed or relieved that the past had deferred once again to the present.

But I did wonder. Was my memory a real one? For so many *had* been—I could feel myself again hiding behind the couch with Emma Louise, sharing pretend scones under the weeping willows, sitting in the grand dining room of the Patterson mansion. Was Morgan's memory a real one? Was *I* the elephant in his memory and *he* the cooing infant in mine? Or had, for a brief moment, two separate memories intersected, like two circles in a Venn diagram, making a shared memory that had never happened?

Morgan and Arnold had moved on to the second verse, their voices now blending in easy harmony. And then I realized two circles had indeed intersected on that fateful afternoon this past August, when a gentleman of a certain age reached for me, feeling briefly he could go home again; and I marveled at how time past, present, and future can lose all meaning and then gain all meaning, in no time at all.

DUMP
At the Church of St. Bernard's
122 West Varick Street
New York, NY

"We will rescue you from the snowstorm of your daily life."
"An elixir just as you feel the frozen tundra may claim you for its own."
"Let good theater lick your wounds and deliver you to a new delirium."

Arnold Freitag
Artistic Director

Constance Wannamaker
Associate Artistic Director

Board of Advisors
Morgan Johansson
Father O'Malley
Jeremy Harrison-Coles III, Esq.

Jeff Ludlow
Technical Director

Barbie Rankin
Secretary/Treasurer

Nathan Emmanuel
Literary Advisor

Evelyn Wambaugh
Musical Workshop Coordinator

Abby P. Rhodes
Venue on the Fringe Coordinator

Cookie Abramson
Concessions

"A not unpleasing amalgam of the daring and the hopeful."—Asbury Park Press

Board Meeting

"Now, this is only my opinion," began Morgan.

"That's what we pay you for!" said Arnold heartily. The group laughed.

"Try some coconut supremes," said Cookie. "They're made with whole wheat and organic coconut."

"They're fabulous," said Arnold. "I'm glad we're taking nutrition into account. Maybe we could get funding for the concession stand."

"I want to do fruit smoothies too," said Cookie. "And maybe something with sea legs."

"Great!" said Arnold. "Here, Nathan." And he generously apportioned two coconut supremes on a napkin with the ubiquitous cup of coffee. We were at our first board meeting of DUMP, and while I was terribly nervous in my capacity as literary manager, Morgan had assured me I was supremely qualified for the job, what with thirty years of reading behind me.

"But not *plays*," I had countered as we made our way briskly to St. Bernard's in the lovely New York City twilight.

"Even better," Morgan said.

"Why?" I pressed.

"You start with a tabula rasa."

I wasn't sure if a blank slate was the best thing an advisor could bring to the table, but decided it wasn't anything I could change now as I bit nervously into my coconut supreme at this, my first board meeting ever.

"Okay," resumed Morgan. "I'm thinking we have a couple of mixed messages here."

"How so?" asked Arnold, now all business, his coconut supreme put to the side in favor of the reverse sides of Xeroxed copies of *Moon for the Misbegotten*, upon which he was prepared to write down everything Morgan said.

"You have several affectionate and original sentences which play on the salubrious effects of a St. Bernard, which is an excellent metaphor for theater. But maybe we should choose *one*."

"Right," said Arnold. "Less is more. We can vote on which one we want."

"Good," said Morgan. "However, DUMP still remains a mystery for the uninitiated." He paused. "Actually, it remains a mystery for everyone."

"We could spell it out," suggested Cookie. "Don't Under Mine Peace."

"Yes we could. We certainly could," said Morgan. "But why?"

"Why?" asked Cookie.

"Yes. First of all, 'undermine' is one word."

"Oh!" said Cookie.

"I know," said Arnold. "I—we thought it would get more attention that way. You know, a play on words. Well, in this case, a play on *a* word."

"Which is cool because we do *plays*," added Cookie earnestly.

"Of course," said Morgan quickly. "But what does it mean?"

"You mean metaphorically?" asked Arnold.

"Let's start with literally."

"It means 'don't get in the way of unwarlike attitudes,'" offered Jeff, a very kind and gentle young man with a gash over his left eye from an accident incurred while playing Paris in *Romeo and Juliet.*

"Okay," said Morgan slowly.

"Like . . . don't fight," offered Cookie.

"Uh-huh," said Morgan.

"It means 'Don't become a mindless member of a society that worships the Military Industrial Complex threatening to overtake this nation and all nations if we don't step up to a higher level of consciousness and say NO,'" said Constance, who had remained quiet up until now, her gaze intense through her horn-rimmed glasses.

"Wow!" said Cookie. "That's big!"

"Yes, it's big. And if we, as artists, are not about to assume the mantle of change, then who will? Who in God's name will?" Constance shouted. "Sorry, Father."

Father O'Malley nodded.

"Constance and I met in a political ethics course at Berkeley," offered Arnold.

"You went to Berkeley?" asked Morgan, displaying more astonishment than was perhaps politic.

"For one summer. My van had broken down."

"Ah," said Morgan.

"So I don't see what we have to talk about. That's the mission statement of the theater company. There's no discussion," said Constance.

"All right," said Morgan gently. "But tell me how *From Bard to Verse* fits in with that."

"Oh, *From Bard to Verse*," Constance scoffed. "That was fluff."

"Fluff," repeated Morgan quietly. I tensed.

"Yes. It was Arnold's baby, and we like to let Arnold do whatever he wants as a kind of payback for all he does as artistic director."

"I see."

"Constance will be directing *The Ancient Samovar*, adapted by Nils Woodhall from the short story by Nikolai Nikimovich for our next offering, and it promises to resonate with all the vision and mission that is DUMP," said Arnold.

"I see," said Morgan again, and I could feel his terror. For to have signed on with a group of artists who had the heart and panache that was exhibited in *From Bard to Verse* was one thing, but to have to work shoulder-to-shoulder with a mean-spirited nitwit like Constance was quite another.

"Constance has her MFA in directing and her doctoral thesis in Russian history," said Arnold proudly. "We're really fortunate that she can fit this production in. She has to get to the Kansas City Theater Center immediately after for the world premiere of the musical version of Camus's *Exile and the Kingdom*."

"Uh-huh," said Morgan evenly.

"Where's Abby?" asked Arnold. "She should be here in case we have to vote."

"Abby should be here, period," said Constance vehemently. "I'm assuming she'll grace us with her presence as soon as her driver can buck all that Fifth-Avenue traffic."

I looked quickly over at Morgan and could see him mentally depositing Constance into a pool of quicksand.

"But, Morgan, let's address the issue of the mixed messages here," said Arnold. "You're basically saying that the meaning of DUMP needs to carry the day more, that perhaps we took flight with the metaphor of the St. Bernard and need to get back to a more cogent statement vis-à-vis not undermining world peace."

"Well, that *or* going with what seems to be the truly uplifting image here—which is that theater can heal. Healing as you did so well, Arnold, with the laughter and tears and awe you provoked in your *fluffy* evening of Shakespeare." Morgan's impatience was thinly disguised; however, no one seemed to notice. For which I was grateful, as Morgan's combustible nature seemed to have come closer to the surface these days than in days of yore.

"Uh-huh," said Constance. "A sort of *kinder, gentler* theater company." Her voice was heavily coated with sarcasm.

Morgan's response was cut short by Abby suddenly bursting into the room.

"Hello!" she said breathlessly. "I'm so sorry, traffic was dreadful!" And she peeled off her velvet gloves and settled into a beanbag chair while Constance thrust a knowing look into the center of the table.

It seemed to me that Abby's entrances were always to be explosive events, perhaps owing to the intense energy of the woman herself— an energy tamped down excessively by Jeremy. Or perhaps this was my own prejudice. Or perhaps it was my writer's eye taking down situations and layering them with far more urgency, far more angst than was really there. No doubt I was in fact being unfair, and Jeremy actually had a calm, gentle, and generous nature that I simply had not been privy to.

"Okay, everyone, let's *get the lead out!*" shouted Jeremy, entering unexpectedly and likewise peeling off his gloves and settling down. "First off, I've got a block of five hundred tickets bought by the Russian Tea Room, another block bought by St. Vincent's Hospital for the employees' Christmas party, and a check being written *even as we speak* by Samuel Rosenzweick for the exchange project with Kiev."

"Coconut supreme, Jeremy?" offered Cookie.

"No. Now I'm going to need a final copy of your mission statement for funding purposes."

"Cookie, I would love one," said Abby quickly, taking two.

"Darling, please, I only have ten minutes here and then I need to get some real work done," said Jeremy, implying that being kind to Cookie was a hindrance to that intention.

"Hello, Nathan." Abby smiled a dazzling smile at me. "Hello, Morgan."

"Hello," Morgan began, but when no sound came out, he cleared his throat and began again. "Hello."

"What did you think of *From Bard to Verse?*" she asked shyly.

"Darling, time, time, time!" reminded Jeremy in what he probably thought was an affectionate tone of voice.

"Arnold," said Morgan gently, "I believe you were very successfully conducting this meeting."

"Oh. Well actually, Jeremy, we were in the midst of coming to terms with our letterhead."

Jeremy glanced over the letterhead. "Looks great. A little wordy though. Maybe get rid of all these quotes—it looks like an ad for a B and B in the Alps or something." He laughed.

"As I told Arnold, I thought *From Bard to Verse* had some of the most original, courageous, and heartfelt work I had seen in quite a while," said Morgan. "Also, not incidentally, a lot of genuine talent." This said directly to the purple eyes of Abby.

"The mission statement, *please?*" said Jeremy, checking his Rolex. He had not bothered to take off his cashmere coat, either having forgotten it in the enthusiasm of the moment or, what I rather suspected, because it enhanced his image as a mover and a shaker in the corporate world.

Barbie—a small young woman whose head had been bent over her yellow legal pad from the beginning of the meeting as she earnestly and frenziedly took down every word—continued to scribble madly while her other hand went through a folding file, whipped out the mission statement, and handed it to Jeremy, no doubt writing as she did so: "Jeremy Harrison-Coles asked for the mission statement at this time, and Barbie Rankin (Secretary/Treasurer) handed it to him."

Jeremy read it aloud. "DUMP is a small nonprofit theater company dedicated to artistic growth in and around the community by stretching the artistic muscles of its members and developing new works which speak to the soul of the collective humanity, where the new voice of the artist can find itself and seek fulfillment while making the world better and ending grief and intolerance. We do this through a main stage series of old and new works, a workshop series for the future main stage series, a reading series for the future workshop series, an arts-in-education program, and an exchange program planned for Kiev." Jeremy looked up and nodded. "Great. Now, Connie, tell me a little about *The Ancient Samovar*," suggested Jeremy. No artiste-speak, just something that will sell me on the production. Pretend I'm a moron."

As Morgan took an intake of breath in preparation for what might be a less than politic rejoinder, I said quickly, "Set in the wealthy Russian home of Bezimenovowich in late-nineteenth-century Russia, a disguised prince, a Cossack, an actress, and a student unexpectedly meet and familial and political loyalties collide and change forever. An unexpectedly vibrant, compelling, witty, and heartbreaking look at the end of one world and the beginning of the next."

There was a silence but for the whisper of Barbie's number 2 pencil.

"You actually *know* this short story?" Connie asked, awed.

"Well," I said modestly, "not in this particular translation."

"Okay," said Jeremy. "Yadda-yadda-yadda, etc. Compelling, witty, heartbreaking, vibrant, unexpected. Great. I'm out of here. I'll see you tonight, babe. Remember, we're meeting the Potters at eight at Lutèce." And he kissed Abby briefly, gave a wave, and was gone.

"We're really very fortunate to have Jeremy on our board. He has raised a lot of money for us and kept us *au courant*," said Arnold.

"Uh-huh," said Morgan.

"But, Morgan, getting back to this mixed-messages thing. How could we clarify?"

As Morgan is not a patient man and hates getting back to a subject, I was a bit anxious to hear what he would say, especially as both Connie and Jeremy had begun to wear on him considerably.

"Change the name of the theater company."

"To?" asked Constance icily.

"The Company at St. Bernard's."

"Oh, how wonderful!" exclaimed the padre.

Arnold nodded. "It has a certain ring to it."

"It's like . . . it's like so much about where we actually *are*!" added Cookie enthusiastically.

"I like it a lot. It reminds me of that dog on Topper," said Jeff, lighting up for the first time.

"Neil," nodded Arnold.

"Yeah, Neil. And it has kind of a warm sense of rescue, of refuge, of safety."

"A pretty far cry from cutting edge," said Constance.

"Not if refuge is understood as the cutting edge it actually is," said Abby.

"Meaning?" said Constance edgily, as if to dare Abby to get in the ring with her advanced degrees from Berkley.

"Meaning that everything has become so glib and harrowing, as if meaning can only be derived from intellectual gambits, from shock effect, from directorial vision that seems myopic at best."

"If you are referring to my production of *Startuffe* last year—"

"Constance, if you still can't see that putting *Tartuffe* on the moon was a mistake—"

"Just because of *one* reviewer."

"Audiences weren't fooled, Connie. Heck, even the *company* wasn't fooled." She turned to Morgan. "Character names were changed. Orgon was Oregon, Dorine became Della Ware, costumes were contrived out of the maps of the states, except Tartuffe who, of course, was wrapped in tinfoil—"

"Milar spandex," said Connie through gritted teeth.

"And the whole thing had to do with America's certain destruction if it remained obsessed with the Space Race."

"Constance thought there was a parallel between that seductive possibility and the religious cant that Tartuffe spins," added Arnold.

"Uh-huh," said Morgan, who now looked extremely pale.

"I think Morgan's right," said Abby. "It's time to admit who we are and what we do. We are a bunch of actors who hope to create moments of transformation for ourselves and the audience. And serve fabulous confections at intermission," she added, taking another coconut supreme and smiling at Cookie. "In this day and age, to create a refuge, to feed the soul and body, *is* to do cutting-edge theater."

"Why don't you just admit you are still miffed that I didn't cast you, Abby?" demanded Constance.

"Miffed? Constance, I continue to be *relieved*."

"Abby, it comes as no surprise to me that you have abdicated any passion for our group," said Constance with a terrible ring of challenge in her voice. "I mean what are the stakes for you if we succeed or fail? How will that impinge on your beautiful life on the Upper West Side?"

"I have plenty of passion, Constance! I have so much passion that I don't need to manufacture it out of TINFOIL!"

"Okay, maybe we better take a break here," said Arnold.

"And as for success or failure, it will depend on whether we can first and foremost entertain people!" Abby continued.

"So why don't we just sit around and read the *Reader's Digest* out loud? That seems to fascinate a huge percentage of Americans!"

"I have no doubt, Constance, that if someone presented you with a musical adaptation of the *Reader's Digest*, you would consider it *cutting edge* enough to produce."

"Just five minutes and we can come back," said Arnold, endeavoring to muster a lighthearted authority.

"Abby, why don't you just stick with your role as the venue-on-the-fringe coordinator?"

"Okay, Connie, as long as you'll stick with yours and just *assist*."

"OKAY!" boomed Arnold. "Jeff, how about another pot of coffee and we can all take a stretch."

"Arnold, maybe this is the time to make the announcement," said Constance.

"What announcement?" asked Jeff. We all paused in our motions for which, only an instant ago, we were immensely grateful.

"Arnold!" Constance prodded.

"Okay. I'm stepping down as artistic director at the end of this season. But rest assured, *The Ancient Samovar* is still going forward."

"Why, Arnold?" asked Cookie, suddenly distressed. "You're not ill or anything, are you?"

"No. No, nothing like that. It's just . . . it's just that I need a break. I need to get up to my parents and help them out a little bit with the tree farm and so on."

There was a pause in the room, a pause that spoke of a surprising sadness at the thought of this gentle and rumpled young man's sudden absence from our lives. I wondered if it had anything to do with what Arnold had confessed to us in Connecticut. I wondered if he was looking for an escape from the beautiful young woman who now looked at him with sudden and gentle love.

And now Cookie suddenly reached out and took Arnold's hand. Arnold reflexively began to pull away, but Cookie held on with surprising determination. The two held each other's eyes. I hoped with fervor that the rest of us were dissolving from their sight.

"Good lord, Arnold! Finish your announcement!" barked Constance.

"Oh. So Constance will be taking over."

There was a second pause.

"I quit," said Abby promptly, and she gathered her things. "It was very nice sharing this evening with you, Nathan, Cookie, Morgan, Father." She looked at Morgan, inhaled as if to say something, thought better of it, and was suddenly gone.

"Abby! Abby, wait! Abby!" Arnold quickly followed her.

Constance leaned back in her chair and put her hands over her eyes. All that could be heard was the whisper—of Barbie's pencil. Her lips moved as she wrote: "Ar-nold-an-nounces-he-will-step down-as-art-i-stic-di-rec-tor-Ab-by-quits-leaves-Ar-nold-runs-af-ter-her-Con-stance-leans-back-there-is -a-break-in-the-meet-ing."

Barbie put her pencil down and looked up and around for the first time. I wondered what life was like for her in the present rather than in the arrival of the present on paper a few seconds later where it had already become the past for the rest of us. She blinked and seemed to notice her coconut supreme for the first time. And then she noticed me. She blinked a second time.

"You're an elephant."

"That's right," I congratulated her. She was interacting for the first time this evening.

"I should put that in," she murmured and quickly went back to her notes.

I mused on whether this was the curse of every writer: to eschew the present so as to rearrange it and live the shadow life of creation. Is this why Socrates disdained the written word? I shivered and felt my own passion for writing to be suspect. I looked over at Morgan, for I felt he would be able to clarify these thoughts for me in the gentle and compassionate way he had, but saw that his right hand was now squeezing his forehead together tightly in a gesture that could only mean a terrible headache was coming on.

"Christ, he's still not over her," muttered Connie to Barbie. "Sorry, Father."

Father O'Malley nodded.

"Over her?" Morgan, Cookie, and I asked at the same time.

"Yes, they were quite an item before Jeremy."

"Were they?" the three of us asked in various degrees of astonishment.

"My god, it's like a Greek chorus in here!" shouted Constance.

Barbie picked up her pencil.

"THAT DOES NOT HAVE TO BE IN THE NOTES, BARBIE!" shouted Constance.

Barbie put her pencil down. "Sorry, Connie," she said.

"I don't know why you insist on writing every word down. It's not as if you're a *court reporter* or something."

"But I *am* a court reporter," said Barbie earnestly.

"Yes, darling, you're a court reporter—but not *here*."

"Okay. Why are you so moody, sweetie?"

"I don't know. I'm tired." Connie kicked the leg of the table and began to pout.

"We'll get you home and into a warm tub, and I'll whip up that beef stew you love."

"With new potatoes?" asked Connie, not looking at Barbie.

"With new potatoes and then some lemon meringue pie."

"Hmmmm."

"And then we'll get you into bed."

Morgan's head hit the table.

"FATHER, I WONDER IF YOU HAVE ANY IBUPROFEN?" I shouted. Everyone jumped, especially the padre, who had been looking over the mission statement, seemingly oblivious to the warm, connubial, and frankly mouthwatering conversation going on between Constance and Barbie.

"You know, I think we do, up in the rectory. Are you ill?"

"No, but Morgan is."

"No, I'm fine," said Morgan, embedding his knuckles into his eyes.

"Morgan, you are *not* fine! Your migraine is coming on, and then tomorrow will be so difficult for you and—" I stopped suddenly, wondering if we were now sounding like Constance and Barbie. And if we were, should I be terrified, or had I misjudged Constance and Barbie? And even if I *hadn't* misjudged Constance and Barbie, and even if I *shouldn't* be terrified of my consuming concern over Morgan, perhaps we were becoming a bit too much like the *Odd Couple* by dear Neil Simon, and perhaps Morgan and I should think seriously about getting some women into our lives pronto.

"I'll go and check," offered Father O'Malley.

"No, Father—" started Morgan.

"No problem!" And Father O'Malley was off.

"I'll go with you, Father," I said, deciding to leave Morgan with Cookie, with whom he could either commiserate or begin something—that is, if Cookie decided to leave Arnold to his worries over the Cracked Plate and embers of a romance long past.

As I trotted out, I reflected that this moment seemed to be a repetition of that glorious evening at Madeleine's, where I had left Morgan to the charms of three lovelies and ultimately landed us in this very evening by my innocent conversation with Arnold. However, I felt I had learned from that evening and that I could be trusted not to get us further embroiled in any misadventures. For one thing, the padre was certain not to have any champagne in his rectory, and I firmly believed—erroneously as it turned out—that such imbroglios were merely the fault of demon liquor.

*   *   *

"Oh, Father, what an interesting life you have led!" I exclaimed as I looked at the photographs on the walls of his cozy study while he went through various desk drawers looking for some ibuprofen.

"Oh yes. I have been blessed," he answered. "Aha!" He picked up a bottle, but then he read it carefully, "Expires July 1986."

"That's probably done for," I said gently.

"Right, right, but I know . . . I'm certain I bought some not so long ago. I just always think it's important to have pain remedies available, since so many people come in with pain."

"But isn't it more of a *spiritual* pain, Father? People certainly don't think of you as a local pharmacologist."

"Yes, I know what you mean," Father O'Malley said vaguely, but he had by now turned to a box of assorted items behind his desk and unpacked them: a Mr. Potato Head, a map of the 1964 World's Fair, the collected poems of T. S. Elliot, a Scrabble game, a picture of himself with Pope John Paul the First, a chess set, a mug from the USS *Constitution*—

I suddenly caught up with myself. "Father!" I said excitedly. "Is that you with Pope John Paul the *First?*"

Father O'Malley stopped in his activity and looked at the picture through his half-glasses. "Yes, that's myself and his Holiness. Il Papa del Sorriso."

And indeed, the pope had a beatific smile.

"My *god,*" I breathed in astonished reverence. "That's like having a 1955 double-die obverse penny!"

Father O'Malley emitted a hardy laugh. "Exactly! What are there? About thirty thousand of those?"

"Twenty-four thousand," I said. "All minted one night in Philadelphia."

And the padre continued to chuckle as he went back to his searching. I marveled at the man, that his picture with Il Papa del Sorriso was packed away with Mr. Potato Head. This was something that Morgan would have very much appreciated, and I wished he were here. As if the Fates were at my beck and call, there was a slight tap on the door.

"Enter!" boomed Father O'Malley.

And there was Morgan.

"Excuse me, Father, but I suddenly thought it would not be wise to leave Nathan alone with you."

"Because, no doubt, he would unwittingly sign you up for doing the readings for the next month or put you in charge of the toy drive for Christmas."

"Yes, although I am no longer certain that 'unwittingly' is the best adverb to describe Nathan," said Morgan, sighing as he settled into a large and slightly cracked leather chair in front of the padre's desk.

"It is good to keep our spiritual guides on a short leash," agreed Father O'Malley.

Both Morgan and I looked surprised. I? Morgan's spiritual guide? Was it even possible?

"Here we go!" Father O'Malley said triumphantly, finding a bottle of Advil that was not overly-encrusted in dust and lint. He shook two into Morgan's hand and poured him water from a thermos on the sideboard.

"Morgan," I said excitedly. "Look. Here's a picture of Father O'Malley with Pope John Paul the First."

"Uh-huh," said Morgan noncommittally.

"He keeps it with Mr. Potato Head and the collected works of T. S. Eliot."

"Really?" And I could see that Morgan was, in spite of himself, newly impressed with Father O'Malley, as I knew he would be. "Wait. Pope John the *First?*" asked Morgan with the same double take as I myself had experienced not moments before.

"Yes. Rather like having a 1955 double-die obverse penny, wouldn't you say?" Father O'Malley asked with a twinkle in his eye.

"Well . . . I'm not sure about that exactly," confessed Morgan aptly. "Just . . . wasn't he pope for only a few months?"

"Thirty-three days, to be exact."

"My god," breathed Morgan.

"Yes, I was fortunately chosen to say mass with his Holiness. It was extraordinary. You know, you don't necessarily have to *like* the pope or even *believe* in the pope. But the *idea* of the pope—well, that is something else, isn't it? I mean, the Church did its best to continue in the tradition of mythology, didn't it? But then it got terribly off-track by taking it all so seriously. You take away the mystery and you have to fill the space with something else."

"Dogma," said Morgan fiercely through the webs of cranial pain.

"Yes, I suppose so," said Father O'Malley gently, leaning back in his chair and looking up at the pleasantly peeling plaster ceiling.

"The mystery is gone."

"Yes. For the sake of clarity. Otherwise, the Church would be accused of being cultish, unreachable, opaque. But I do agree that in some ways people already have so much clarity, *or think they do*, that they perhaps should not have worship mitigated by clarity. I really don't know. That is why I think your theater company is so helpful."

"My—"

"Because it retains the mystery. It cannot help but do so. Think of it. Two thousand five hundred years—done exactly the same now as then. The same mysteries, fears, passions, courage. Antigone, Creon, Oedipus, Medea, Orestes . . . as valuable now as then. Would a shoe or a sandal be as valuable? Perhaps to a museum. But think of it: a character, his needs, his passions. The *same*."

Before Morgan could respond, astonished as he was to be even *having* this conversation in a cracked leather chair in the office of a Catholic priest, Arnold bounded into the room.

"Christ, she's really gone!" said Arnold. "Sorry, Father."

Morgan stood. Arnold crumpled into the chair.

"Have a couple of Advil," Father O'Malley said, "and we'll talk."

*   *   *

Morgan and I walked home in silence, leaving Arnold to talk quietly and at length with Father O'Malley.

I knew that Morgan's headache was diminishing and his silence was not from pain but from the fact that he was angry. But not at me. For let me assure you, dear reader, that I in *no way* made Morgan sign up to head the toy drive.

"But what could I do?" demanded Morgan. "What with Pope John Paul the *First* and Mr. Potato Head and all that Advil and then Arnold—"

"Admitting to his still-fiery passion for Abby—"

"Then Connie and the dreadful thought of *The Ancient Samovar!*" continued Morgan as if he hadn't heard me.

"And not acknowledging what is past is past and a beautiful woman with excellent culinary skills awaits him—"

"My god, I can see it all ahead of us. It will be five or six hours of impassioned sorrow and whining, and we won't be able to *move* when it is over."

"But if he could just admit it and stop using the cracked plate and a long-finished romance as an excuse and dive into Cookie's inviting and openhearted—"

"And now a toy drive!"

"Well. Yes," I said weakly.

"For a parish of two thousand!"

"But not all of them children, so not all of them needing—"

"Lord." Morgan uncharacteristically sat on the front stoop of a trattoria filled with people delighting in cappuccinos and biscotti. They looked so happy. I sighed.

"Morgan, I guess I was drawn to the toy drive because of the simple fact that I am, in fact, a toy. And the thought of uniting a toy with a child, or a childlike human of any age," I added quickly, "would be a kind of devotion to celebrate."

Something about this rather simple statement of fact (perhaps because it was so truly heartfelt, as statements must be when one has to finally reckon with one's own limits, when one must close up the notion of infinite possibility, when time and space finally become forces that triumph over dreams, when one, in other words, finds the courage to admit that the simple fact of having written a title and three opening sentences may not ever make you a writer) resonated in Morgan, and his stern furrowed brow relaxed. He looked at me almost as if seeing me for the first time. Then he looked at the sky. I looked at it as well. We sat staring for a while although, owing to buildings and the glow of city lights, not many stars could be discerned. I decided to be as quiet and still as possible, for I was finally learning.

"And also, I still find it astonishing that you actually knew the plot of *The Ancient Samovar!*" added Morgan in a seeming non sequitur, yet one I knew born of some not unwarranted frustration with my constant participation in life and Morgan's skittishness about trusting said participation.

"Well, to be honest, Morgan, I don't."

Morgan wrested his gaze from Orion and looked at me. "WHAT?"

"Well, Arnold said it was late-nineteenth-century Russian literature. So I took a stab."

"You took a stab."

"Yep," I said weakly.

Morgan looked up at the stars again. I did so as well, although my neck was beginning to get a bit cramped.

"You took a stab," Morgan repeated softly.

I felt the point had been made, so I kept uncharacteristically silent.

Imagine my surprise, dear reader, when Morgan picked me up and took us into the trattoria and ordered two decaf cappuccinos and a plate of biscotti. Morgan stayed quiet, although not moodily so, and I munched as softly as biscotti will allow.

Then Morgan took out a pad and pen, cleared his throat, and said, "All right then, Nathan. Let's take a stab at this toy drive, shall we?"

The Ancient Samovar

(MASHA AND ANDRE ALONE ON STAGE)

Masha: Oh, but I cannot stand my life, Andrushka, for it eats and eats away as time hangs so heavy. I have nothing! I believe in nothing! I am but a horrible swamp, infested with the dire bleak awareness of my limited days on earth—the vapid desert behind me, the dark empty waters ahead. What is there left for me but to wait? To die? OH WHERE OH WHERE IS NICHOLAS STEPHANOVA NICHOLA?

(ENTER MOTHER)

MOTHER: Andrushka! Bring the samovar! The ancient samovar!

ANDRUSHKA: Oh, Mother, how stupid you are! Tell Sonia, our serving girl, to bring the samovar, the ancient samovar. I will not bring the samovar, ancient or otherwise. I am not a servant. I must go instead to the university. And my foot hurts.

MOTHER: Tell me of Moscow, my dear son, my dear one, Andrushka.

ANDRUSHKA: Oh, Mother, shut up about Moscow! Every day you say "Tell me about Moscow," and I tell you "Shut up about Moscow! Shut up about Moscow!" I say for my foot pains me every day with memories of those stupid student agitations when a cart of chickens was overturned onto my foot.

MASHA: And me? What of me? You speak of the university and your foot and chickens, but what of me? I am your sister, but I am also a horrible swamp, infested with the dire bleak awareness of my limited days on earth! (THE CRIES OF CLOTH MERCHANTS OUTSIDE THE WINDOW ARE HEARD) And the frightful din of these cloth merchants is so tormenting!

ANDRUSHKA: Purge yourself, Masha! Purge yourself of dread and go to the city! Go to the market! Go anywhere, but run! Run, Masha! Run before I tell you to shut up as I tell our stupid mother every day.

MASHA: How dare you tell your sister to run! SONIA! (SONIA ENTERS WITH A BOOK) How dare you read when we, your betters, await the samovar—the ancient samovar! Bring it at once. (ENTER DOSEKIN, DRUNK) Dosekin! Drunk with vodka again!

DOESKIN: Yes, my dear little bird. For once I was in the seminary but am no more. Hello, Sonyushka. Reading again? For what? For what? Will reading help you carry a samovar? I think not! (HE LAUGHS SO HARD, HE FALLS DOWN. SONIA EXITS.)

(ENTER FATHER, WEARING A TOP HAT)

MOTHER: Father! My love, my dearest one, how are you?

FATHER: Shut up, you stupid woman! I am cold and just arriving from the noisy, loathsome factory which makes things I no longer believe in. I will never write another short story. And I see you have bought lump sugar again, you stupid woman! Where is the samovar?

MOTHER: FATHER, DO NOT SPEAK AGAIN OF THE LUMP SUGAR! DO NOT, OR I WILL KILL MYSELF. OH WHERE OH WHERE IS NICHOLAS STEPHANOVA NICHOLA?

(ENTER NICHOLAS STEPHANOVA NICHOLA IN A SOLDIER'S UNIFORM)

FATHER: How dare you enter our home, Nicholas—we who adopted you when you were an infant and clothed you and cared for you while you paid us only thirty rubles a day for our love—how dare you enter dressed as a Cossack! Take off your hat! Take off your hat, or I will not be able to forgive this transgression!

NICHOLAS: Father, hear me.

FATHER: Do not say "Father, hear me." Do not say "Father, hear me" wearing that hat, for your mother has bought lump sugar again. I will never write another short story, and the samovar—the ancient samovar—has still not made an appearance.

NICHOLAS: Hello, darling Masha. Hello, dear brother Andrushka. And at once, I must say good-bye.

MASHA: GOOD-BYE? WHAT DO YOU MEAN "GOOD-BYE"?

NICHOLAS: Calm yourself, dear Masha.

MASHA: Do not say good-bye, Nicholas, for I love you.

(ALL GASP)

MOTHER: (NERVOUSLY RUBBING HER HANDS TOGETHER) Where oh where is the samovar?

(ENTER SONIA WEARING A HAT AND COAT, CARRYING THE SAMOVAR)

NICHOLAS: Do not say you love me, darling Masha, for I love Sonia and we are to be married.

(MASHA FAINTS. NO ONE NOTICES. ANDRUSHKA POURS HIMSELF A GLASS OF TEA.)

ANDRUSHKA: (DRINKING) At last!

NICHOLAS: We are leaving. No need to see us to the door.

(NICHOLAS AND SONIA EXIT. MASHA REGAINS CONSCIOUSNESS)

MASHA: NICHOLAS!

FATHER: SHUT UP! I will go to the factory. (HE PUTS ON HIS HAT) For I see now. (TEARS IN HIS EYES) Through my grief, I see now it is only there I will find peace and quiet. It is only there that my true work can begin.

(HE EXITS. MASHA HOLDS THE SAMOVAR TO HER CHEST AND HEAVES HER CRIES TO THE GROWING DARKNESS AS LIGHTS GO TO BLACK.)

In the sudden inky blackness, I felt a ray of hope. This could very possibly be the end. I held my breath. I prayed. I had almost given up hope when suddenly, the house lights popped on. Morgan and I were momentarily blinded. I wanted to turn to him, to see if he was still alive; but it was impossible to move, frozen as I had become in that final stage one reaches at times in the theater. I had passed through the first five stages: (1) Dread that things may not improve, (2) Realization that things will not improve, (3) Fear that we may not be able to make a graceful exit at intermission, (4) Realization there will be no intermission, (5) Fear we had died and not lived an exemplary enough life, and (6) Being at peace with that fact for, if one were to use Dante's version of hell, this wasn't too bad. Close though.

So it was indeed a happy shock to discover I was actually alive and still had time to atone. I assumed the feeling was the same for Morgan. However, our potentially shared happiness was now mitigated by the immediate gathering of the sweet and overtaxed actors at the stage edge, all with hopeful expressions.

But what could we say? What could *anyone* say after what we had just been through? There was only one thing *to* say, "Cancel while your reputations are still intact."

I wiggled my ears to get some feeling back in them and waited to see how Morgan would phrase the above sentiment.

"Good! Good work, everyone! Very, very fine commitment to text and situation. Why don't we all take five minutes and stretch before we go any further."

Arnold nodded. "TAKE FIVE, EVERYONE!"

"Oh, thank God!" said Cookie. "Because I really have to pee. Arnold, I don't think I'll keep drinking tea all the way through. I mean I thought it was a good idea at first because you said to keep your lives going on offstage so that we can come *from* somewhere and then go *to* somewhere which—wow, it's actually a lot like life—but I think I'm going to have to think of something else for Sonia to do. Maybe her nails. Maybe she has like a small hair salon in the back of the dacha."

"Great!" said Arnold, all business. "Keep exploring, that's what this is all about. Keep *exploring*."

Cookie scampered to the bathroom. Arnold turned to us.

"Morgan, where would you like to give notes?"

"Uh, actually—"

"Maybe right up here on the stage and everyone could just cluster around. Would that be okay?"

"Sure. Actually, I don't have many—"

"JEFF, BRING STAGE LIGHTS TO HALF!"

"Stage lights to half, roger that," called Jeff, who was both the stage manager and Andrushka.

"Arnold . . ." Morgan began.

"Let me get you some coffee, Mr. Johansson. And you too, Nathan."

I nodded my head stiffly.

"Morgan, is this hat just too extraordinary?" asked Evelyn, coming on with the enormous black hat with the plume and black netting she had worn as Madam Arkinyashaka, the mysterious mistress of the old doctor—both of whom we had met years ago, it seemed.

"Evelyn, the hat is lovely, bold, eerie. No, I definitely love the hat," said Morgan, leaping with relief at having a genuinely positive thing to say.

"Tell me honestly," Evelyn whispered. "Are we *dreadful?*"

"No! Not *at all!* No, not dreadful *at all.* No no no no! Not a bit!"

I thought sadly to myself that Morgan would have to do a *lot* better than that for anyone to believe him.

"I believe you," said Evelyn, grasping his arm and then moving away to unfurl her netting.

Morgan answered my unspoken astonishment. "In situations like this, hope will always override reason. And that's not such a bad thing," he added, more to himself than me.

"Uh-huh," I said, slowly working my jaw.

Arnold rushed up to us with coffee and a plate of Russian tea cakes. My mood began to improve.

"I had no idea, Mr. Johansson, that when I suggested we do a run-through without stopping that it would take close to six hours."

"Right," said Morgan, gingerly standing up. "That's something we'll have to address."

"The thing is, Connie never did a run-through. She has a way of working that is really intense. Like they'd rehearse opening a letter and putting down the letter opener then someone entering and looking for a hat then someone pouring tea, then she'd do it over and over with different rhythms while tapping her pen."

"I see."

"I think it gives everything more depth. Maybe. I don't know! I don't know!" He ran his hand through his full head of hair causing some of it to stand up, making him look like a cockatiel.

"Anyway, when she got the call that they were starting two weeks earlier at the Kansas City Theater Center, she said she'd leave it in my capable hands. But honestly, Mr. Johansson, I really think I'm out of my depth here. I mean, I was never very smart in school. The closest I got to college was when my van broke down, and I honestly don't know how I've even gotten *this* far." Arnold was gesturing wildly with the hand that held the plate of tea cakes, and four of them tumbled to the floor.

"I mean look at all this! Father O'Malley and Father Fernando being the cloth merchants, and this great space and these actors, and Evelyn Wambaugh and my *mother* coming in at the last minute to play the mother when Barbie left with Connie, and Cheryl doing amazing work weeping over the samovar—I don't even *get* that, but I guess it brings us back to the title. And Jeff who is so pathologically shy being willing to play Andrushka, and you and Nathan and—"

I was beginning to get the terrible feeling we were once again to be launched into the frantic infinity of prose which I had thought blissfully behind us and quickly found a fallen Russian tea cake to elevate my falling blood sugar.

"And, well, Cookie." And his eyes gazed at her as she sat with Cheryl who was still on the floor holding the samovar, but now laughing with Cookie about something. Probably how amazing it was that "tea" rhymes with "pee." I sincerely wanted to join them.

"I mean honestly, Morgan, does it get any better than this?"

Morgan looked at all that Arnold had just described. "It most certainly does not," he said thoughtfully.

"But between you and me, and Nathan of course—"

I nodded my interest from the floor, my mouth full of tea cake.

"It's really bad, isn't it?"

There was a long pause. The fact was, the posters and programs were printed, there had been an article in a grocery circular, Jeremy had booked the opening night party at the Russian Tea Room, there was an unaccountable number of seats already sold, and a grant was pending. Morgan took a breath. I stopped chewing; so tense was I in anticipation of the next moment when truth must be told.

"TIME!" called Jeff. "NOTES, EVERYONE! ON THE STAGE! GET PADS AND PENCILS!"

Morgan dutifully came onstage and sat, and everyone immediately and happily gathered around. I wondered if St. Jude, patron saint of lost causes, had much on his plate right now.

Morgan began. "All right. First off, again, let me congratulate you. I truly think it's an achievement when such dense and complex material can sound so natural, so honest. I believed each and every one of you, and that is no small accomplishment considering this is a 1952 English translation of-of . . ."

"A short story by Nikolai Nikimovich," I said quickly.

"Thank you, Nathan, exactly. Which is about . . . which is about . . ."

It was frightening to see Morgan stymied. I handed him a Russian tea cake and smoothly continued, "The once-wealthy-but-now-fallen-upon-hard times home of Bezimenovowich in late-nineteenth-century Russia."

Morgan nodded enthusiastically while managing another tea cake and drinking half his coffee.

"Exactly, Nathan. Yes, thank you. My goodness, these cookies are *fantastic!*"

"Yea, Cookie!" Cheryl called out, and everyone clapped. Cookie looked down, radiant at her culinary victory.

Morgan clapped along with everyone else. When everyone had stopped clapping, Morgan continued, stopping at last when he realized they all were waiting patiently for his thoughts.

"And the truth and energy you have all managed tonight is truly noteworthy."

"Yea, truth and energy!" Cookie said, and everyone began clapping again.

"Good. So that being said, I wonder if we could take everything you've done so far, and what we're going to do now, just as an exercise of course, what we're going to do now is allow it to be a sort of . . . well, for want of a better word, a screwball comedy."

The suggestion was met with silence.

"A what?" asked Evelyn. "I'm sorry, I was still untangling my netting. What did he—"

"He said a *screwball comedy*," said Jeff guardedly.

"You said a screwball comedy—right, Mr. Johansson?" asked Arnold. "But did you mean screwball as in *screwball*? Or screwball as in the more tragic connotation of screwball?"

"I mean like . . . like the Marx Brothers."

"Uh-huh," said Arnold thoughtfully. "But do you mean the Marx Brothers as in the *Marx Brothers*, or do you mean Marx Brothers as in the more tragic—"

"Arnold," said Morgan levelly, "there is no tragic connotation to the Marx Brothers."

"Oh my god!" said Cookie, hitting her head. "He means like *Marx*! You know, the guy who invented Communism! My god, that is so brilliant that I'm glad I am sitting down!"

Everyone suddenly looked relieved.

I felt a sudden hysteria at the sheer inanity of the suggestion. I was terrified I was going to guffaw suddenly and uproariously and inappropriately.

Arnold's mother, Pat, guffawed suddenly. Everyone looked at her.

She calmed herself at once. "Oh! Oh, I am sorry, but I guess I must be seeing it. Already."

"Really?" asked Arnold and Morgan.

"Really," Pat answered. And she looked at Morgan fondly, seeing his concept as something that might not be possible but was definitely kind. And kindness in the long run, she knew personally, counted for much more than simple success.

"You know, Mr. Johansson, that's actually a *concept*!" said Arnold. "We could hang some red flags, we could paint the entire stage red for that matter, we could—"

"No."

"No?" asked Arnold.

"No, Arnold, because I mean exactly what you are all afraid I mean. Whatever picture you have of a screwball comedy: heads banging under tables, people falling on banana peels, running in and out of doors, water squirting out of flowers in lapels, feet getting stuck in buckets, and so forth. Arnold, you and I will have to put our thinking caps on now. In fact, maybe everyone has some ideas."

The room was silent.

"Or perhaps everyone would like to go home and sleep on it."

No one wanted to move.

"Morgan?" asked Cheryl, flicking the bangs out of her eyes.

"Yes, Cheryl?"

"Why do you think it could be a screwball comedy?"

This was the question I had also been wanting to ask.

"Oh well, because as I tried to hear the actual lines, that is as I *heard* the actual lines—they struck me as incredibly funny. It was a thorough revelation. It was as if the great Anton Chekhov himself was sitting here with us, enjoying a colleague's work."

He gestured to the folding chairs. We all looked out with him then returned our attention to Morgan, who continued to look upon a smiling Mr. Chekhov only he could see. Sensing finally that the cast was not going to be satisfied with the invocation of a Russian genius, even if he was sitting there giving them a ghostly thumbs-up, Morgan sighed and returned his attention to the silent and expectant group of actors before him.

"Right. So if we could speed up the glacial—that is, if we could *halve* the running time, then . . . you see?" Morgan smiled and looked out at all of us, solemn, still, expectant. "What I *mean* is, with the incredible *intensity* of the situation where *nothing really happens* because the expected visitors get lost in the forest and one person's foot is rendered useless when it is run over by a cart of chickens, and another loses his regiment and the first floor of the villa gets taken over by singing cloth merchants, and Sonia never puts down the samovar until the last moment—well, I mean you see?"

And perhaps it was precisely because *none* of us were seeing anything whatsoever, but earnestly so, that at this moment, Morgan, without any preamble whatsoever, without even the smallest of giggles, suddenly pitched into a fit of hysterics like I had never seen. It made his response to Arnold's cooing infant look like a snicker.

We waited, thoroughly awed.

Morgan wiped his eyes. "Sorry. Excuse me, but I just find the situation genuinely—"

But the hysteria would not be tamped down. He shook with laughter, he wheezed, he cried, he doubled over, the paroxysms would not be stopped. Finally, he came up for air, wiped his eyes, blew his nose, took a deep breath, and looked at us solemnly.

"Fu-fu-FUNNY!"

And he was off again, only this time in his weakened state, as he clutched himself and doubled over, he fell out of his seat and onto the floor.

"Jeff?" said Arnold, with a voice that suddenly assumed command of the situation.

"Yes, Arnold?"

"From now on: decaf."

"Check," said Jeff, writing it on his clipboard.

We all continued to watch solemnly, for Morgan was not a man to be incontinent with his laughter by any means. He was a man of gentle decorum, as if he might be a guardian of the world's treasures and thus could not leave his post of sobriety for long. Knowing that he had already done so not long ago during Arnold's imitation of the cooing baby, tonight's display could only herald a new chapter in this stoic man's life. If the chapter meant an asylum, I hoped he could have visitors.

"You know," said Evelyn, "I always thought that 'rolling in the aisles' was a bit of a hyperbole."

"And a total exaggeration," added Cookie.

"But if we could do *that*," said Evelyn, looking at Morgan.

"We'd be a hit," said Arnold quietly.

"God, a hit," said Evelyn reverently, her eyes going inward to the memory of *Kiss me Once, Kiss me Twice.*

"A hit, Cheryl! Better than *Radio City's Christmas Spectacular* because we'd be *individuals*," said Cookie, crossing her impossibly beautiful legs.

"A hit," said Jeff who had been in theater for twelve years now with only a gash to show for it.

"A hit," repeated Arnold, thinking of how beautiful it would look on the marquee. Thinking of actually *getting* a marquee.

"A hit," said everyone to themselves, for they were none of them too young to understand the miracle of those two words; how they justified all the years, dashed hopes, training for good or ill, all the auditions, the abuse, the neglect, and finally the choices they had made once at a fork in the road, where the unlived possibilities of another life had haunted them ever since.

Morgan was now lying on his back, all laughter finally purged, staring up at the eight rudimentary stage lights fashioned out of paint cans, which even at half their brightness glowed with possibility.

"A hit," he said softly.

Mr. Fredericks

We hopped out of the cab at Forty-Fifth and Ninth and, sure enough, there was the Good Time Charley's as Sadie had described. Perhaps because I am not prone to bus trips, the restaurant did not have the same deleterious connotations for me that it had had for Sadie. Looking through the vast window, its copious salad bar and checkered tablecloths seemed quite inviting. I looked hopefully at Morgan in case he was thinking that a burger and fries with a pitcher of sangria would go down well right about now, but he was distracted by the enormous hustle and bustle of pre-matinee mayhem.

"My god, we live in pastoral isolation compared to this!" exclaimed Morgan as we made our way through the tidal wave of oncoming theatergoers.

"So much hope, so much eagerness," I said, remembering fondly the evening of *The Heiress.*

Morgan made himself as narrow as possible against the side of the restaurant as thousands of little girls appeared from around the corner, racing to the Martin Beck Theater for *Annie.*

"Aren't they sweet?" I said, gazing out from the safe compartment of Morgan's pocket, remembering my darling Emma Louise.

"Uh-huh," Morgan said noncommittally.

"And just think, Morgan. In about ten years or so, many of them may be attending the National Academy of Drama, inspired perhaps by the magic of today."

"Uh-huh," said Morgan.

"And perhaps you might ask one, 'So, Amelia, when did you get interested in the theater?' And she'll say, 'Well, when I was a little girl, my mother took me to see *Annie* early in November. In fact, I remember exactly. It was November 16, and I can even remember streaming forth with all the little girls in my school, and oh! In fact, this is peculiar, but I even remember there was a very kind gentleman with an elephant stuck in his pocket, and I suddenly had a bit of a frisson, although too young to know the word at the time. And now, today, you remind me—'"

"There he is!" said Morgan, for once completely disinterested in my narration.

We dove across the street in the path of several irate drivers and approached a gentleman who stood on the corner, wearing a tattered coat, a cap with a pom-pom, and with his feet slipped into shoes as if they were slippers. He held out a cap and jangled it with what can only be described as a sort of charismatic hope.

"Excuse me, sir, but may I ask if you remember helping a woman into a cab about a month or so ago and giving the driver money?"

"You certainly may." The man smiled.

"All right, then. Do you remember helping a woman into a cab a month or so ago and giving the driver money?"

"Yes, I do."

"Then you are he."

"Yes, I am. Yes, sir. I am, indeed, he."

"May I ask what led you to do that, sir?"

The man thought. "What or who?"

"All right then, who?" asked Morgan, steeling himself for the typical acknowledgment of God, my Lord Jesus, Allah, and the like.

"Sir Isaac Newton!" said the man. He paused. "It's a punch line, but I can't for the life of me remember the setup."

Morgan smiled and relaxed somewhat for, while the answer might have been insane, at least it wasn't religious.

"May we buy you lunch, sir?"

"I wouldn't say no to a good lunch, sir. I wouldn't say no."

And we crossed back this time in a more decorous fashion and into Good Time Charley's.

The maître d' approached us with a grim look. Morgan smiled charmingly. "Table for three, please. Nonsmoking."

We settled down to anticipate the arrival of Cokes and burgers, Morgan nixing my suggestion of a pitcher of sangria as this was to be a business meeting. We introduced ourselves.

"Douglas Fredericks. Very kind of you, this."

"A kindness repaid."

"Better it be just a kindness."

"All right," agreed Morgan.

"There is too much currency already. Or not enough," he added ruefully, glancing at his hatful of change.

"I'm wondering if you would like a job," said Morgan.

"A job?" asked Mr. Fredericks.

"Yes. As a sort of caretaker, technical director, night watchman, and handyman for a small theater company that works out of a church."

"Sounds like a lotta jobs."

"You are correct. But it is, technically, only one job at a time."

"Why me?"

"Because you helped that woman into the cab."

"Uh-huh."

"There are certain things you would have to perhaps learn how to do—electrical, mechanical, and so on. But these are all doable, learnable things," said Morgan in what was, for him, severely dilapidated prose.

"I see."

"We can offer you a salary and a room and kitchen privileges at the church. It might be a nice way to live. To earn a living."

"Yes." He thought quietly for a moment, chewing on a breadstick. "And it probably wouldn't hurt anyone."

"No," agreed Morgan, puzzled. "No it probably would not."

The man was silent for a long while, his eyes gazing out the window and up to the sky. Our burgers came. We ate contentedly in more silence. Morgan sipped his Coke and eyed the gentleman curiously. Evidently, Mr. Fredericks had much to consider. Finally, Mr. Fredericks took a deep breath. Morgan and I leaned forward slightly.

"Would you like my coleslaw, Nathan?" he asked.

I was astonished for, while I always want more coleslaw, I thought I had cured myself of covetous glances.

"I—I would, actually."

"Take it."

"You give a lot away," said Morgan.

Mr. Fredericks seemed to consider the statement. "Yes." He paused. "You're asking a lot," he said.

"I am?" said Morgan, surprised that his offer had turned into a request.

"Yes."

"How so?"

"Do you think I could have some cheesecake?"

"Of course!" Morgan ordered three cheesecakes and three coffees.

We ate in silence. We sat in more silence. Luncheon patrons had left long ago for the theater or business. Waiters reset tables for dinner. They put candles out. They hovered officiously. Morgan made no move to nudge the situation along. I sipped the remainder of my Coke through the straw and made slurping noises. The sun began to set.

"Will there be anything else, sir?" the sleepy and somewhat truculent waiter asked.

"Are you closing?" asked Morgan innocently. "Do you need the table?"

The waiter sighed, looked at his cohorts, rolled his eyes at the total ennui of the situation, and said disinterestedly while looking out the window, "I merely wondered if there will be anything else."

"Yes, there may be actually *anything else*," said Morgan. "There may be dinner. We may begin with drinks and move on to steaks and potatoes and go to the salad bar twice and have hot fudge sundaes. We may go to the phone and invite sixty or seventy people to join us. Buses may arrive. We may have a wedding here. There may, in fact, be a great deal of *anything else*. Who knows?"

Truculence is one of many raspberry seeds in Morgan's wisdom teeth.

"Ah!" the waiter chirped, and with his eyebrows thoroughly arched, he sauntered back to his cronies.

I liked Mr. Fredericks. I liked that he weighed his options, for every move brings a tearing away of the familiar. Who knows what comfort his corner brought him—the ceaseless passing of other lives, the occasional added jingle to his coin cap. He'd be leaving a job that kept him out of doors and the suspense of not knowing where his next meal would be coming from. He would have to spruce up his attire, get work boots, be on time, fix things, listen ceaselessly to "bring the samovar, bring the samovar, bring the samovar." His corner, at least, brought independence and an iconoclastic poetry into his life.

"Okay," he said finally.

The silence had gone on so long that Morgan and I both were quite startled to find ourselves finally answered, and in so simple and friendly a way.

Morgan shook his head slightly. "Okay?" he asked, astonished.

"Yep. Okay."

"Well then. Perhaps you would like to come to rehearsal tonight at seven to check out the facility and meet everybody."

"Okay."

"Okay then."

And Mr. Fredericks rose with grace, shook our hands, bowed slightly, and left. We followed him out and brought our bill to the register. After paying, we returned to the table to leave the tip and were shocked to see that Mr. Fredericks had already placed a fifty-dollar bill under a water glass.

Morgan and I looked at each other in astonishment.

"I hope this job won't be a step down for him," I said.

"The man is a mystery," Morgan agreed.

As we settled into the cab which would bring us back to our pastoral isolation, I glanced out the back window, giving a final look of affection as is my wont to all places where something large has happened, even if the largeness has not yet been processed in a cognitive way. The sun was casting its final sharp rays into the avenue and all was achingly beautiful as New York can often be— seeming itself to notice that at least one world, and maybe many, had changed today.

Several More Surprises

We arrived at the theater at St. Bernard's to discover that Arnold had coffee ready and Cookie was putting out a lovely array of date-nut bars and chocolate truffles.

"If this is any indication," I said to Morgan, "we're going to have a great rehearsal."

"Uh-huh," said Morgan grimly. For truth to tell, he was still not certain how he had gotten himself into this particular project and in all fairness could not blame me this time. Although in more fairness, "this time" probably would not even exist were it not for my conviviality at Madeleine's party. Although to bring all this fairness to a conclusion, I had never had champagne before that evening.

"I'm thinking, Morgan, that I'll start a line of baked goods and call them 'Cookie's Cookies.' What do you think?" asked Cookie.

"I think it's an excellent idea," responded Morgan courteously, if a bit automatically.

"It's more than excellent," I said earnestly, having just bitten into a truffle. "You will make the world a better place."

"Oh, Nathan! You are the sweetest thing!"

The other actors were all arriving, greeting each other, kissing and hugging the way actors do.

"Morgan!" Arnold came over to us. "I have some good news and some bad news. What order is best for you tonight, considering what lies ahead and your particular sensibility?"

"Um . . . I think the bad news first."

I understood Morgan's reasoning. He already felt fairly close to bottom. Might as well hit it thoroughly and then hope the good news came with a lifeline.

"Okay. Well, my mom had to drop out. We got an emergency call. My dad had an 'episode' at the tree farm." Again, Arnold used his fingers to indicate the finger quote, this time rolling his eyes as if to indicate profound annoyance with his father's insanity.

"Oh, Arnold, please don't be annoyed with your dad," said Cookie. "I'm sure he just forgot to take his meds. It can happen to anyone. I mean, my mother was convinced she needed to see a foot doctor, her feet were so bad. Then she discovered she had put her orthotics in upside down."

"What?" said Arnold, astonished. "How—how do you know?"

Cookie shrugged. "She told me."

"No, I mean about my dad."

"Oh, your mom and I really hit it off. We talked about all sorts of things that night I made paella."

"You did?"

"Of course, I made the paella."

"No. I mean you guys talked about—"

"Sure we did. I mean bipolar's the kind of thing you can discuss even if you have to measure carefully. Oh! Hello!" Cookie called, seeing Mr. Fredericks looking about in the doorway, maybe suddenly wondering how *he* had gotten himself into this particular project.

"Would you like some coffee and cookies? I'm Cookie, and this is Arnold. Morgan said you would be dropping by tonight."

Mr. Fredericks looked at Cookie as if he was seeing an angel— which of course, on a certain level, he was. We had already become so accustomed to Cookie's beauty and openheartedness that sometimes it took a stranger to remind us. I looked over at Arnold to see if this was the sort of kick in the head he was waiting for. But it was always hard to tell with Arnold whether or not he had just been kicked in the head.

"Thank you, Cookie," said Mr. Fredericks. He had certainly spruced up nicely, wearing a pair of khakis, a flannel shirt, and work boots. The interesting thing, however, was his clothing did not have the telltale signs of brand-newness: the horizontal creases in the shirt, the pants too crisp, the work boots unscuffed. He looked like he was wearing clothes he actually owned.

Morgan looked at Arnold. "I would very much like to hear the *good* news now, Arnold," he said evenly.

"Oh, right." Arnold was still looking a little dazed from discovering his mother had openly discussed the cracked-plate situation with Cookie, and Cookie had given the information about as much importance as the new sandals for spring. Actually, less.

"Oh! Right, I almost forgot. Mr. Fredericks, you'll probably want to see this also."

And he guided us to a corner of the theater which contained, as far as I could tell, a huge pile of metal rubble.

"Oh my god," said Morgan.

"Nice," said Mr. Fredericks, nodding.

There was a moment of awe shared between the two men which, for me, was completely unaccountable. I waited for enlightenment.

"What you are looking at, Nathan," said Morgan, "is a collection of twelve resistance dimmers, twelve Fresnels, eight Lecos, and piles of cable—all of which, if installed properly, will enable the theater space to have a myriad of lighting possibilities, will enable it to be the place of magic it deserves to be." He paused, amazed. Then returning to reality, he said, "Arnold, where did you *get* this?"

"A theater company up in Connecticut was closing, so I . . . we"—he gestured to Cookie—"went up and bid on it today."

"It was awesome!" Cookie said. "I got to drive a van! With a stick shift!"

"And what did you pay for it?"

"About $957. Which is an incredible bargain—don't you think, Morgan?"

"I do indeed, but how does the theater have $957? Seeing as we made, after expenses, about $36 from the last show?"

"*From Bard to Verse*," I explained to Mr. Fredericks.

"Good title," he said thoughtfully, chewing on a date-nut bar.

"Oh, we had it," said Cookie. "I saved a lot from being a Rockette."

"That is incredibly generous of you," said Morgan.

"Oh well, I love . . ." She looked at Arnold. "I love the theater, I really do." And she blushed a deep red.

If Arnold did not get down on his knee this minute and propose, I would.

As if reading my thoughts, Morgan said quickly, "Cookie, Arnold, I wonder if I may have a moment with Mr. Fredericks."

"Sure, Morgan," said Arnold, and he gently led Cookie back to the coffee table. I could see the two of them in earnest conversation. I prayed it had more to do with spending the rest of their lives together rather than with Arnold's suggestion of substituting spelt wheat for all-purpose flour.

"Mr. Fredericks—"

"Douglas."

"Douglas, I haven't a clue what to do with this. Do you have an idea?"

"I think I can figure this out."

"I mean we would need I haven't any idea what: circuit breakers, outlets, plugs? I don't know—"

"I think I can handle this."

"And then we'll have to deal with codes and probably *inspections*." I could see Morgan bristling the way he does with rules of any type.

"Mr. Johansson—"

"Morgan."

"Morgan, you have to hear me: I can handle this."

"Yes. Thank you. We all live on a wing and prayer. This is the theater. But there is reality. Like I said, codes and inspections and—"

"Morgan, I was an engineer. At NASA."

Both of us stood, stupefied. It explained a great deal in an odd way, but not enough for us to find our voices. Mr. Fredericks smiled.

"I know. How could an engineer at NASA wind up on the corner on Forty-Fifth and Ninth? I was involved with the *Challenger* disaster. Minimally so, but how do you calibrate minimal with a disaster that could have been avoided at many different steps along the way? Is this what happens to the mind, to the soul, when one becomes part of an assembly line? Is integrity inevitably going to be lost? And is one grateful when it is? I haven't been able to get the pain of those questions out of my head since. Which I suppose is one way of saying for a while there my marble bag wasn't tied too tight."

"Oh," said Morgan.

"But, finally, craziness can sometimes be just an excuse for a vacation. I had no idea the lady with the Elvis head would bring me here. But here we are, and there we go."

I thought this an excellent summation of all that had happened since Morgan found me in a flea market, for was I not the equivalent of the Elvis lamp? Although, on further consideration, I truly hoped I was one or two steps up.

"My god," said Morgan. "Indeed, here we are. And there we go."

Mr. Fredericks eyed what still looked to me like a huge pile of metal rubble.

"Piece of cake," he said quietly to himself.

*   *   *

The rehearsal was a long one, filled more with hope than any indication the production would avoid being an unmitigated disaster. Our taxi ride home was silent, as we mulled over our individual thoughts. I was still musing on Mr. Fredericks, on the excellent truffles, and to be honest, at the enormous challenge that Morgan faced with his concept for *The Ancient Samovar* and his group of willing—but, for the most part, *hapless*—thespians.

Where Morgan's mind was, I cannot say. Perhaps the challenges he faced were somewhat mitigated by the fact that Arnold's mother's leave-taking had given him a practical reason to call Abby, which he had done immediately upon leaving Mr. Fredericks to further examine the lighting equipment.

"Hello," said Abby upon answering the phone.

"Hello, Abby," said Morgan. "This is Morgan."

"Hello, Morgan," said Abby solemnly. "This is Abby."

"Yes, of course. Hello."

"Hello."

"How are you?"

"Fine thank you, and yourself?"

"Fine. Thanks. Listen. I know this comes out of the blue, but Barbie had to leave the production because Constance was called into Kansas City two weeks earlier and—"

"I'll be there in twenty minutes."

"Okay, but I want to warn you I'm putting in a lot of pratfalls. Especially for the mother."

"*Pratfall* is my middle name."

"Funny."

"I agree. But it also happens to be true. Southern thing. Long story. Time for that later. I've got to find my knee pads." And she hung up.

Of course, it could be that Abby was a woman who was wired to take necessary action at any time, day or night. Or it could be that Abby was ready to come to Morgan at any time, day or night. I sighed, seeing another couple skirt about their love for each other. Then again, who was I to criticize? For I had dillydallied around Doris so long, she had become engaged.

"Nathan, I know this is none of my business," said Morgan now as we motored along in our southbound cab, quiet but for the soft swaying of prayer beads on the rearview mirror. "But the fact is . . . the fact is that I really never saw you and Doris as a couple."

"Really?" I said. For while this statement carried a bit of pain, it also let me off the hook from the dire results of my procrastination.

"I just think you are not an elephant of procrastination. That is not your fatal flaw."

"You may be right, Morgan. I would hope we only get one fatal flaw, and mine seems to be rushing in where angels fear to tread."

"There is an inner wisdom that guides our actions, Nathan."

Any further thoughts were cut off by the cab's arrival at our door. Morgan paid the driver a large tip, and we started up the stairs. I was musing on the thought that I might have inner wisdom and found it comforting, if a bit unbelievable. When we reached our door, there was a cardboard box with a UPS sticker on it. Morgan looked at me.

"Honestly, Morgan, I have no idea."

"I believe you," he said, hoisting the box and letting us into the apartment. He set it on the table. "It's addressed to you," he said.

For indeed it was. "Nathan Emmanuel c/o Morgan Johansson."

Morgan got out his penknife and carefully cut away the tape. The cardboard box yielded yet another box with one-inch-diameter holes cut in its top and sides.

"I'll be damned," said Morgan.

"What?" I asked.

"Go ahead," he said, lifting off the top.

I peered inside. There was a mound of hot pink tissue paper and an envelope addressed to me. I opened it, unaccountably shaking.

> Dear Nathan,
>   Yes, of course that was me at Café Des Artistes. While my leave-taking must have been quite dramatic for you, I assure you all is well. All in a day's work.
>   If the beret, the kindness Marissa extended to you, your excellent French, and the concentration you exhibited over your writing are any indication, your life is full. As for myself, I majored in literature and was on my way to a PhD in medieval studies when my life took an unexpected turn. I cannot tell you anything more about myself because those are the rules of the game. I probably will not see you again, but wanted to give you this.
>   With all my love that never wavered,
>   EL

I blinked back tears.

"It was she! Morgan! It was indeed she!"

"Yes," said Morgan, truly astonished.

"And now she is gone. Oh, Morgan! Is this kind of love even *worth* it if it brings so much pain?"

"I think you will find it is, Nathan. For surely this box filled with pink tissue paper was not meant simply to send you a note."

"Oh."

Suddenly, we heard a delicate sneeze come from within the box. Quickly, I removed the paper. What greeted me was so astonishing, I would have fallen off the table had Morgan not been there to keep me steady. For an angelic (there is no better adjective) pink-and-white seersucker elephant with soft pink velvet ears, luminous button eyes, and startling eyelashes peered up at us. She sneezed again. Then she smiled.

"Thank goodness it's *tissue* paper," she said. "Hello. You must be Nathan. My name is Genevieve. Emma Louise sent me. I do hope I have not come at an inconvenient time."

I will say this, dear reader, uncategorically and without apology: there is no inconvenient time to fall irrevocably in love.

Opening Night

While I am certain I have demonstrated a clear respect for my mentor, for both his knowledge and wisdom, I hope I have communicated also the carefulness with which Morgan lived his life—fully, yes; with commitment, yes; but within a confines that had remained strong and familiar for many years.

Needless to say, turning *The Ancient Samovar* into a screwball comedy was—though not *technically* impossible—certainly beyond anyone's attempts heretofore to illuminate a 1952 English translation of a short story by a Russian author no one had ever heard of.

With twelve moderately to magnificently gifted actors.

In a church with a stage the size of a walk-in closet.

In a week.

I couldn't help but wonder if the magnificently rewired lighting system might be the finest thing the audience would experience tonight.

"You doing okay, Nathan?" asked Mr. Fredericks as he passed me at my station at dimmer 1.

"Fine," I said tremulously.

"Piece of cake, little guy." Mr. Fredericks smiled at me. "You were brilliant in last night's rehearsal." And he was on his way to put touch-up paint on the troika that would make a sudden—and hopefully comic—appearance at the end of act 2.

For indeed, I was suddenly on the "lighting crew" because Arthur, an intern from the High School of the Performing Arts, had come down with the flu. My nervousness at being such an important part of the performance knew no bounds. It is one thing to be a literary advisor, to say such obvious things as "The Russians had *glasses* of tea rather than cups" and so on, but it is quite another to be a pivotal member of the performance team. For when Jeff called "Light cue number 1 moonrise on a ten-count—go!" my job was going to be to pull the lever of dimmer number 1 down (on a ten-count), which would thereupon allow Sonia to say the first line of the show, "Will you look at that moon rise!"

"Morgan," I pleaded, "couldn't I be in a cue that was part of a simple interior? For no one ever said, 'Will you look at this simple interior light up so beautifully!'"

"No," Morgan said briefly, as it seemed Cheryl was suddenly having trouble with her roller skates.

"But—"

"You'll be great, Nathan. You were great last night."

"But—"

"No buts, Nathan!" And he was off again because Evelyn wasn't certain if she was supposed to come in from upstage right and run downstage left in scene 3 or enter downstage right and exit upstage left in scene 4. Or both. This was a more pivotal concern than might at first be recognized, as Morgan had shaved three hours off the play simply by having the actors do the entire play twice as fast. While this required everyone to know all their entrances and exits perfectly (and stay out of the way of wildly oncoming people as they strove to make it back on stage within seconds) and left everyone panting by the end, it certainly aided in the screwball genre that was Morgan's vision. Added to that, of course, were such touches as giving roller skates to Sonia, having Evelyn sing all her lines in a specious bel canto style, making Andrushka fall down each time he entered and exited owing to his broken foot, and a myriad of other touches too numerous for me to mention now, as I am currently having palpitations over my pivotal role in the proceedings. For, dear reader, the moon had to rise *ten times* during the performance.

The fact of the matter was that we had all lost track of whether any of this was actually funny. We were exhausted, nervous, hopeful, and vaguely nauseous. Indeed, the only one who seemed truly in his element was Mr. Fredericks, but I suppose working at NASA prepared one for such extremes.

"Half-hour, Nathan," whispered Jeff. "I'm opening the house."

"Uh-huh," I said, wishing desperately I was anywhere but here.

"Kisses, everyone!" called Cookie.

"Break legs!" added Cheryl.

"Merde!" called Evelyn as she sprinted to the green room.

"Nathan, can I try the water trick out on you?" asked Oscar.

"Go right ahead," I said. "For how bad could—"

"Thanks! It works!" said Oscar happily. And he ran off to join the others, leaving me to wipe the water from my leatherette and to make sure my headset had not shorted out.

Now I could hear the audience entering and chatting over the strains of *The Living Balalaikas Play Your Favorite Jazz Standards*. Indeed, Arnold's ability to find the most unlikely components in this city knew no bounds, illustrated this moment by Morgan giving actors a final pep talk and myself sitting on this stool in total readiness, my trunk coiled around dimmer number 1. I released the lever briefly to peer around the curtain, and indeed, the house was filling quickly. I could see Jeremy welcoming people as they arrived—my god, was that the *mayor*? And there was Father O'Malley in his cloth merchant costume greeting parishioners, looking as if he could burst with joy. There were all our friends from the Studio Coffee Shoppe, Doris and the gentleman whom I assumed was her fiancé, and Mr. Turnip Head. There was Sadie and what looked like four of her children with their dates. There was a bevy of beauties who must be Rockettes, there was Marissa with a charming gentleman, and there was Veronica, swathed in yet another set of scarves with at least five members of the National Academy. And there was Genevieve, looking radiant in the first row, engrossed in her program. Of course, she looked up at that moment and smiled directly at me before I ducked back behind the curtain. I returned to dimmer number 1 now with a profound sense of peace and joy.

For what difference could it possibly make if the moon rose too slowly or not at all? What difference, really, if I or any of us did not prove to be perfect tonight? We already *were* perfect—if this audience was any indication, if this hard work and belief in each other were any indication, if the resurrection our souls had experienced by agreeing to believe we could do it was any indication, if everyone's love sat patiently reading the program was any indication. If all this could happen in a small crowded room in a church in New York City at the end of the second millennium, then we were all already perfect.

So it was no surprise when Jeff quietly spoke into my headset, "House lights to half, preset to half, house lights out, preset out, cue 1 moonrise on a ten-count—go!" that the moon rose perfectly, with no effort on my part whatsoever.

*   *   *

NICHOLAS: Do not say you love me, darling Masha, for I love Sonia and we are to be married.

(MASHA FAINTS. NO ONE NOTICES.)

(AUDIENCE LAUGHS)

FATHER: Oh beast! That you should not ask your father who loves you more than life itself?! (PAUSE. THOUGHTFULLY) And how will we live without your thirty rubles?

(MORE LAUGHTER)

MOTHER: Oh brute! That you should marry a serving girl and tell this to your mother! (PAUSE. REMEMBERING) Who is already sick with grief at having bought lump sugar! (MOTHER BURSTS INTO TEARS)

(AUDIENCE HOWLS)

ANDRUSHKA: Can this night get any worse?

(MOTHER RUNS OFF WITH HER APRON TO HER EYES. AS SHE ARRIVES AT THE DOOR, SONIA ENTERS WITH SAMOVAR, CAUSING THE DOOR TO SLAM MOTHER INTO THE WALL BEHIND IT.)

(AUDIENCE IS OUT OF CONTROL)

SONIA: Hello, darling Nicholas!

ANDRUSHKA: The Ancient Samovar at last. (HE RUNS TO IT. FALLS DOWN.) THIS BLASTED FOOT OF MINE!

(AUDIENCE GASPS FOR AIR)

ANDRUSKHA: (STILL ON THE FLOOR) My mind is made up. I will teach at the university for it is the only thing I am good for. (HE STARTS TO DRAG HIMSELF OFFSTAGE THEN STOPS.) Oh, what really is the use? (HE STAYS ON HIS BACK STARING AT THE CEILING; FATHER IS STARING OUT. MASHA IS STILL UNCONSCIOUS.)

NICHOLAS: (CHEERFULLY OBLIVIOUS) We are leaving now, dear family. (NO ONE MOVES; NICHOLAS STARTS OUT, TURNS, HOLDS UP BOTH HANDS.) Please. No need to see us to the door.

(GASPING LAUGHTER FROM THE AUDIENCE)

(HE AND SONIA LEAVE. CLOSE DOOR. MOTHER IS STILL BEHIND IT, SHE SLOWLY SLIDES DOWN THE DOOR TO THE FLOOR.)

(AUDIENCE IS ROLLING IN THE AISLES.)

(EVELYN ENTERS DRESSED ALL IN BLACK WITH THE LARGE LOVELY HAT AND NETTING WRAPPED ABOUT HER, CARRYING AN ACCORDION. SHE BEGINS TO PLAY "I LOVE PARIS IN THE SPRINGTIME." MOON RISES, AND THEN, AS IF IT THINKS BETTER OF IT, SETS. LIGHTS FADE FINALLY TO BLACK.)

The applause began immediately. It can only be described as an explosion of appreciation. The actors came out all together as a company and took several bows, the applause growing even more. Then, unaccountably, we were suddenly all onstage together: myself, the three interns who ran lights with me, Jeff, Mr. Fredericks, and finally Morgan—a man, up until now, comfortable only in the shadows.

Together, we took a ragged and good-natured bow.

And then the audience, almost as one, bolted to its feet, giving this young and insanely optimistic company a standing ovation. Not the usual standing ovation where a few people stand, and then others behind them so they can see the curtain call and then the rest so as not to be thought curmudgeons. No, this was a hearty endorsement given us by the entire audience. I say *almost as one*, because one person stood seconds before the rest. And no one was more surprised than me to see that it was Jeremy.

Finale

We were all gathered in Morgan's apartment, making posters for St. Bernard's toy drive.

"I'm so concerned about the title," I said woefully.

"The title?" Morgan asked.

"Yes. It is so cumbersome."

"I would say instead *encompassing*," said Abby.

"What do you think of my flyer, Evelyn?" asked Arnold, as he passed out coffee and banana-nut bread.

Evelyn began looking for her reading glasses in her capacious handbag, finding instead a long lost hat, which she placed on her head with triumphant joy.

"This bread really rocks, Arnold," said Cookie. "You are a totally fast learner."

"Thanks, Cookie," said Arnold. "Maybe you shouldn't worry about whether the title reflects the book at all, Nathan. Maybe you should call it—"

"*Reality: The Next Step?* Or *Sidewalks Give Perspective?*" I suggested.

"Holy cow!" said Arnold. "Those were the two *exact* examples I was going to give."

"No way!" said Cookie.

"Is anyone else getting a feeling of déjà vu?" asked Arnold.

"I don't know about that, but I sure feel like I've done this once before," said Cookie, shivering.

"Why, Arnold, it is absolutely lovely," said Evelyn, having found her reading glasses and gazing at the daring magenta flyer. "But I don't think my name should be so big."

"But you're the big name, Evelyn."

"Oh lord, no one remembers *Kiss Me Once, Kiss Me Twice!*"

"They will," we all said as one.

We looked at each other in a moment of silent surprise.

"Hey! Whatever happened to Constance and Barbie?" asked Cheryl. "Weren't they supposed to be back after the *Exile in the Kingdom* gig?"

"Oh well, Constance felt the theater was not going in the direction she had hoped," said Arnold.

"You mean it was becoming increasingly clear, emotional, transformative, and uplifting?" asked Abby.

"She didn't put it in those terms exactly. Fact is, she is going to become the new artistic director at ACT in San Francisco."

"Couldn't they come up with a better name than *that* for a theater?" scoffed Cookie, outlining the words "TOY DRIVE!" with neon-green glitter. "I mean it's a little obvious, even for me."

Abby and Morgan smiled at this. Then they looked at each other and felt their smiles deepening.

"Well! I better get going," Abby said briskly. "I have to meet Jeremy at the Four Seasons. Let me take some posters to put around there."

"Really? Will they let you do that?" asked Evelyn.

"Sure. It was Jeremy's idea, actually. Plus he's buying a block of tickets for your show, Evelyn. He figures he can probably get you into the Oak Room if he gets the right people in to see you."

"I have to confess something," said Arnold. "When I first met the guy—no offense, Abby—but he just didn't seem the type to connect with a ragtag bunch of thespians. Just goes to show you something."

"Uh-HUH!" Cookie nodded emphatically. "He's become a really nice guy."

"I know!" said Abby a little too brightly. "It seems theater can redeem anyone. Everyone." Again she looked at Morgan.

"I'll say. I mean look at us," Cookie said. "*The Ancient Samovar* got a great review in the *Times*, Evelyn is going to wind up at the Oak Room, Arnold got funding from Jeremy's law office, we're giving Sadie a reading of her new play *An Even Dozen: Nothing Remotely Even About It*, we're making posters for a toy drive with this incredible glitter. Oh, and also, I'm pregnant."

For the second time, the room was stilled in silence.

"Yep," said Arnold bashfully, taking Cookie's hand, unmindful that in doing so he had coated his own with cobalt-blue glitter.

"I just had it with all that nonsense about the cracked plate," said Cookie.

After numerous congratulatory murmurs and shrieks at this announcement, Arnold—characteristically wanting to share the spotlight—added, "And Nathan is writing a book!"

"Yes! How's it coming?" asked Abby, donning her lovely swing coat and crushed velvet gloves while gathering up posters and availing herself of one last slice of banana-nut bread, all seemingly in one gracious movement.

"It's finished," I said quietly.

Now the room was silenced for a third time.

"Finished?" asked Abby, choking on her bread.

"Fin-finished?" asked Morgan, his cup of coffee stilled in on the way to his mouth.

"Yes."

"But will the theater really take off?" asked Arnold.

"How will my show go?" wondered Evelyn.

"Will I be a good mother?" whispered Cookie.

"What will my children say about *An Even Dozen: Nothing Remotely Even About It*?" asked Sadie.

"Will we?" said Morgan, looking furtively at Abby. "I mean will I—"

"Will I?" said Abby at the same time, looking furtively at Morgan. "I mean will we—"

"I don't know," I said simply.

"But, darling, shouldn't *you*—of all of us—know?" asked Genevieve gently.

"All I know is this: I don't."

"Well, if it's any consolation, Socrates said he was the smartest person he knew because he knew he didn't know anything," offered Mr. Fredericks, stepping down off a stepladder to pour himself a cup of coffee, having just finished rewiring a drop lamp.

"Oh my god, it's a *total* consolation," said Cheryl.

Morgan and Abby stared at each other, uncertain. Arnold glanced at Evelyn, then down at the new flyer, and finally at Cookie. Sadie looked out the window, seeing the Empire State Building with a new fondness. Cookie gazed at her array of glitter then came to rest upon Arnold's kind and gentle face. Mr. Fredericks stared deeply into his coffee, watching the chaotic patterns of the cream resolve themselves into an order only he could see.

There was now a fourth profound and—I might add—unbearable silence in the room, as if something had changed forever. I suddenly felt responsible and was about to apologize when Evelyn spoke.

"At least we know two things we didn't know before, Nathan. We got here, and we know what we want. The rest is up to us."

I looked upon Morgan's beautiful home and the array of gifted people it held. I thought of how my hope of finding Emma Louise had faded, to be replaced by two gifts only she could have given me: my love of life and the love of my life. I thought of my recent adventures, so opposite to the thirty years I had spent reading about the adventures of others.

And I suddenly realized that all those years in the attic were what I was doing in the meantime, before a gentleman of a certain age found a kindred spirit in a New York City flea market toward the end of the second millennium. Now I—we—had dreams that could become real in this next meantime, if we began to step toward them.

And then I knew one thing with a certainty I never would have thought possible as I looked at all of us, gently embraced by the beautiful sepia-toned light that flooded Morgan's apartment every evening about six—relative, of course, to the earth's rotation and the tilt of the axis.

The meantime is beautiful.